"Christmas is getting better and better!"

At the sound of Matt's voice, Jillian's eyes flew open.

Sunlight streamed through the window, framing Matt's head like a halo. He was lying beside her, fully dressed, his chin propped on his fist. "Did you change your mind about me stepping in for Harry?" he asked, any resemblance to an angel vanishing instantly.

"His name is Harrison, and this isn't what it looks like—the heat is off in my bedroom." Jillian spoke defensively, drawing back to put some space between them.

"And here I'd decided you couldn't resist me." He tried to look chagrined but didn't quite manage it.

Jillian sat up self-consciously, making an attempt to smooth her wildly disarrayed hair.

Slowly the humor left Matt's face and he studied her thoughtfully. "You look like a wide-eyed Sleeping Beauty. Continue looking like that and I have half a chance of convincing myself to keep my hands off you. But it's not going to be easy."

Val Daniels says she'll try anything once, from waitress to market researcher, from library aide to census coordinator. But her real love has always been writing. It's fitting that her first published novel, *Silver Bells*, is a Christmas Romance, because her grandmother used to put Harlequin Romances in her Christmas stocking! Val lives with her husband, two children and a ''Murphy dog'' in Kansas.

SILVER BELLS

Val Daniels

Harlequin Books

TORONTO • NEW YORK • LONDON
AMSTERDAM • PARIS • SYDNEY • HAMBURG
STOCKHOLM • ATHENS • TOKYO • MILAN

ISBN 0-373-03092-4

Harlequin Romance first edition December 1990

For Grandma,
who shared her love of Harlequin Romances
with me.

CHAPTER ONE

"THE KANSAS Highway Patrol has announced another highway closure: Due to blizzard conditions and low visibility, I-70 from Lawrence to Salina..."

Jillian Kemp slammed down her paperback and clicked off the drone of the radio weatherman. That was the third road to be closed in north central Kansas in less than an hour. Should she get out of this backwater cabin now? While she could?

She prowled anxiously to the window. A curtain of snow shrouded the night and she couldn't tell whether it was still coming down or just blowing. She couldn't see her car, parked less than fifty yards away. But then she hadn't been able to see it the last time she checked, either.

She glanced around the borrowed hideaway, pleased with all she'd accomplished during her busy day and reluctant to leave it behind, yet leery of staying.

Holiday warmth radiated from every nook and cranny. If Harrison would just get here, she knew he'd be suitably impressed. She wanted their first Christmas together to be perfect, so she'd come ahead to clean and decorate the empty cabin. He was to have driven down this afternoon after he escaped his office.

So where was he? He should have been here four hours ago. The blizzard busily dumping itself on the entire Midwest seemed to promise she'd spend Christmas by herself, after all.

She bit her lip. She'd only agreed to this premature honeymoon because she couldn't face the holidays alone without Grandma.

The lights flickered and then went off. "Oh, Grandma, haven't you done enough?" she groaned. Grandma had been adamant in teaching her the rights of marriage and the wrongs of skipping the ceremony and going directly to the "fun" part. A guilty conscience wasn't helping Jillian to feel comfortable with her plans. "Please, not the electricity, too."

She waited expectantly for the lights to come on. Instead, the hollow darkness settled in as if it intended to stay.

A soft thud outside, followed by a barely audible oath, sent her flying to the door. Thank heaven! He'd made it. "Go play guardian angel somewhere else," she muttered toward the ceiling. "Isn't it bad enough that I have to do this to keep from missing you so much? Do you have to make me feel guilty, too?"

The latch of the door rattled and Jillian flung it wide. "I'm so glad you're finally here!" she called as a blast of cold rushed at her. A well-bundled figure stepped in, bringing a flurry of snowflakes with him. He closed the door, shutting out the wind, and then she was in his arms.

She cupped his face with her hands and shivered. "You're like ice," she whispered, trying to defrost his ears with her warmth. Frozen crystals showered her fingers as he pulled away. She smiled, not at all surprised at Harrison's reaction to her eagerness. She'd kept him at a distance up to now. But she'd agreed to his idea of an engagement celebration, and she had to start as she meant to go on or she'd be lost. She laughed nervously and entwined her fingers behind his head.

His gloved hands slid gingerly up her arms and he started to ease her away. She pressed her body to the length of his and covered his chilled lips with her own. His continuing lack of response *did* surprise her.

Jillian parted her lips invitingly. This was what he'd been wanting. He was going to get her wholehearted enthusiasm. He relaxed and gave her kiss for kiss until a current of longing, stronger than any she'd known before, swept through her. Her breath mingled satisfyingly with his as she sighed. When she could barely breathe and her grip on him weakened, he raised his head.

A low rumble started in the chest next to hers, culminating in a soft laugh. Jillian froze.

"Santa's already been here, I see," said an unfamiliar voice. "Are you my present? Or did he forget one of his elves?"

The hair stood up on the back of her neck and her heart thundered. She willed herself to move away, but her legs wouldn't obey. The wind rose mournfully, and Jillian recalled her journey down the lonely road leading here. All the cabins she'd passed were closed for the winter. No one would hear if she screamed.

Then she remembered why she'd liked the isolation when she borrowed the cabin. Harrison!

"I'm expecting someone. I thought—" It was obvious what she'd thought, but why hadn't she noticed that this wasn't Harrison? *I have to stand on tip-toe when Harrison kisses me,* she scolded herself. And this man's shoulders were wider. "Would you mind letting me go?"

"I think you've got it backward." The husky voice sounded mocking, and Jillian dropped her arms. His arms circled her again, tightening around her. "But you're wonderfully warm." His words settled into her tousled hair and raised goose bumps down her spine. He moved away a moment later, leaving her feeling chilled and alone.

"What happened to the lights?" He tugged the gloves from his hands and removed his coat. "Did you want to greet your friend in the dark?"

"The electricity went out." She scowled, irritated at herself for answering. It occurred to her that he was probably just stranded and looking for help. "Are you lost?"

"Why didn't you start a fire?" he asked.

"I've tried. It keeps going out." If he was stranded, why didn't he give her a straight answer? His lighter flicked, bringing a spot of brightness into the room. She watched suspiciously as he went to the fireplace and peered in. He rearranged her neatly laid logs.

"What are you doing?" she demanded. He acted as if he were the owner of the place instead of an unwelcome guest. "You can't just walk in and take over," she protested. But she welcomed the steady yellow glow that grew and dimly lit the room.

His medium-length, straight hair trapped the honey-colored light and sent out its own glow. His craggy profile etched itself against the shadows. The ice crystals dotting his neatly trimmed mustache gave his face a tinseled look.

"Who are you?" she asked. Her wariness grew as he ignored her and extended a hand toward the flames.

He continued to frown pensively into the fire. *He's nuts,* Jillian told herself and promptly stepped behind the large couch that separated the main part of the room from the door. "Did you have car trouble?"

He turned, at last acknowledging her presence. "Not exactly," he said. That was all—"not exactly."

She fingered the floor lamp beside the couch. Would it be too heavy to use as a weapon? Then it occurred to her that maybe he'd had an accident. "Would you like to call for help? There's a phone in the bedroom." She groaned inwardly. If he turned out to be an escaped ax-murderer, she'd given away her only hope of being rescued. If he'd been the grim reaper, she'd probably have handed him a butcher knife.

The corner of his mouth curved as if he'd read her mind. "My car will be fine in the ditch for now, thanks." His smile reminded her of Dastardly Dan's as he tied Polly Pureheart to the railroad tracks.

He was definitely an escaped lunatic, she decided. "You can't stay here!"

"I can't go anywhere." He tossed his navy pea jacket across one arm of the couch and came toward her.

Jillian edged away, circling the opposite end of the couch, then shifted from one foot to the other.

"You're beginning to make me nervous," he said.

Trying vainly to keep an eye on him while searching the gloomy room for a promising means of defense, she missed his lunge toward her. Even then she would have evaded his outstretched hand if the coffee table hadn't met her shin with a whack. She yelped as he grabbed her wrist, his hold light at first, then tightening as she tried to hop away. Tears of pain and fear filled her eyes.

"Calm down." He spoke soothingly. Trapping her shoulders between his palms, he turned her to face the firelight. He shook his head warningly as she judged the distance between her hand and the hefty marble ashtray on the end table. "You're scaring yourself, you know. Have I done anything to make you think I would hurt you?"

Just the kiss. But she'd been responsible for that, she remembered. She blinked and drew a long breath. His touch was gentle.

"That's better," he continued as she grew still. He gave her arms a reassuring squeeze. "I don't know any more about you than you do about me, and I have a lot more reason to be suspicious."

She started to protest but he put a finger to her lips.

"Later." He nodded toward the Christmas tree holding its dark vigil in the corner. "You've obviously been here a while. Did you happen to run across any candles? I don't think the electricity will come back on right away. Let's get some light, then we can talk." He released her.

His suggestion seemed logical. Seeing him clearly would help. "I saw an oil lantern in one of the kitchen cabinets."

"Show me." He led her toward the kitchen.

"Oh, no!" Jillian pulled away and rushed to the far end of the counter where her cinnamon-scented wine was still warming, awaiting Harrison's arrival. "I hope this isn't ruined." She turned off the heat. Mundane though the action was, it made her feel she was finally taking control of the situation. Surely she could handle burned wine, no electricity, a blizzard and Christmas Eve with a stranger who might be—no. No sense in scaring herself again. Come to think of it, at least she wasn't alone.

"The lamp was in that cabinet up there." She pointed to a spot above the refrigerator. "You get it and I'll see if I can find some candles." She groped in one drawer, then another.

"Any chance you've seen some oil for this?" he asked close to her ear a minute later.

She jumped, banging her wrist, and he laughed aloud at her oath.

"I shouldn't let you have this," she said, irritably rubbing her forearm. She slapped the flashlight she'd found in the drawer into his hand and indicated the utility closet. "Try there."

He switched on the flashlight, shining it directly in her eyes. "Batteries seem fine."

Pushing his arm away from her face, she squinted to readjust to the dark.

"Sorry,' he muttered absently, then swung the light back under her chin. Jillian flattened herself against the sharp edge of the counter top as he propped his hand beside her and leaned in, the light's width away.

His face was golden. Gold hair, gold eyes—tiger eyes—gold complexion. Why hadn't she noticed the tickly-looking mustache when he kissed her?

"You even look like a Christmas present," he said, eyeing the red bow she'd tied around the collar of her white jumpsuit. "What's your name?"

"Does it matter?" she asked defensively.

He shrugged and moved to the closet. "Thought it might be nice to know, since it looks like we're going to be sharing this cabin for the next day or two."

"Listen, you can't just walk in some place and announce that you're staying. I won't throw you out to freeze to death but—" She knew she sounded ridiculous, when he smothered a laugh. He wasn't a big man, but he had a good eight inches on her. And he had gall. She didn't have any trouble imagining him throwing *her* out.

"My name's Matt Carson," he said, continuing the conversation from behind the closet door. Shutting it with his foot, he placed a bottle of lamp oil on the counter beside her.

"Are you going to ignore everything I say?" she demanded.

"Why don't you take some of those candles into the other room and light them?"

He'd done it again. She wanted to shake him.

"And I sure could use some of your mulled wine."

"But—"

"Humor me?" He passed a hand through his hair, leaving his damp hair disheveled. "I'm not going anywhere, and I don't figure you are, either. We have at least two days to hash this out. Can we do it later, when we can actually see each other?" His voice softened and Jillian felt a caressing quality in its tone. "First things first, okay? Then I'll answer all your questions."

He looked exhausted, she noticed with a twinge of sympathy. She sighed, shoulders sagging, and gathered the paraphernalia she'd unearthed in the drawer. "Do you have a match?"

He reached in his jeans pocket and produced a lighter, which he tossed to her. Then he turned to carefully fill the lantern with oil.

"It's probably undrinkable by now," Jillian muttered a little later as she placed mugs of mulled wine on the table. Then she sank into a chair beside the fire, surveying the room. Candlelight almost reached the corners. Ornaments glimmered. She caught her breath. Even without the glow from the strings of tiny lights she'd arranged so meticulously, the tree cheerily dominated the room.

With shattering clarity, she remembered her grandmother's wry voice, repeating her standard comment after the decorations were hung. "Christmas was prettier before electricity."

Jillian had always suspected that judgment had more to do with their sickly-looking trees than with electricity. Still, she had to admit the greenery over the mantel looked lusher than it had earlier that day. The two stockings hanging there cast a surreal shadow, and she felt like part of a life-size Christmas card. The nubby brown couch looked inviting instead of drab; the mismatched chairs looked intimate.... But she was sharing it all with a stranger!

"I know you did this, Grandmother," she whispered sternly. She imagined she heard a mellow laugh. For the first time in the four months since Grandma's death, Jillian didn't gulp back tears just thinking about her. She was too irked at her meddling. *But what did you do with Harrison?* she wanted to ask.

She turned her watch toward one of the candles.

"It's not quite midnight." Matt's voice startled her. *Quit sneaking up on me,* she thought. "Thank you," she said.

"Anytime." Matt placed the lantern carefully amid the greenery on top of the mantel and lowered himself into the other wing-back chair.

"Nice," he commented as he took a sip from his mug and settled deeper.

Her patience snapped. "Look, Mr. What-ever-the-heck-your-name-is—"

"Matt."

"I've been as patient and hospitable as I can. It's cold and nasty outside, it's Christmas Eve and all of that, but don't you think you owe me some kind of explanation? Maybe we can find someone to help you get your car out of the ditch so you can be on your way to wherever you were going." She consciously slowed down, leveling her voice, which threatened to become shrill. "I've gone along with you up to now because I assume you're lost or something. I ought to be terrified—"

"Are you?"

"Not anymore, but that's beside the point." Losing the rhythm of her speech, she stopped and glowered at him.

He leaned toward her, resting his elbows on his knees. She had his full attention now and wished she didn't. His warm eyes were hypnotic.

She jerked her gaze back to her wine, sniffing indignantly. If she didn't look at him, he couldn't get her offtrack. "You waltzed in here like you own the place—which you don't. You act like you plan to just hang around—which you can't. You even hinted that you think I might need to be watched or something. A friend of mine lent me this cabin, and I'm sure she wouldn't appreciate my filling it with anyone who happened to drop in." She made the mistake of glancing up again.

He smiled.

"Stop that," she hissed. Couldn't he be serious?

The corner of his mustache quivered as he raised a brow and replaced his grin with a mock-serious look.

That exasperated her. Praying for composure, she decided to use the same tack she would with one of her boss's difficult constituents. "Perhaps it would help if I knew where you were headed. Won't someone be worried? Isn't someone expecting you for the holidays?"

"I was coming here."

She wanted to hit him.

"The light threw me off because my friend's cabin is the last one on this lane. I saw the light and assumed there was another cabin farther on. I went right past, down the boat ramp. I ended up in the ditch to avoid the lake."

"You must have taken the wrong road," she offered pleasantly.

He shook his head. "Afraid not. I came here fishing last summer. This is the cabin we stayed in."

Jillian's voice rose an octave. "You've been here before?"

He nodded. "I think *you* settled into the wrong cabin."

Jillian sat back, stunned.

"Don't worry. I'm not going to throw you out." He glanced around. "Especially after all the trouble you went to." There was no question about the mockery in his expression now. "As anxious as I was to escape all of the Christmas routine and spend some time on my own, I have to admit, it's kind of cozy."

CHAPTER TWO

DON'T PANIC. DON'T PANIC. Jillian couldn't breathe.
No wonder Harrison hadn't arrived. She'd probably
sent him to some cabin miles from here. He was
probably at the right place—mad with worry—
stranded by the storm, and without a key to get in.
He'd freeze!

Did she take the wrong road? Jillian wrinkled her
brow. Karen's instructions had been very detailed.
Jillian had followed them to the letter.

"But my key fit!" she suddenly remembered.

"Maybe the cabin wasn't locked," he suggested
helpfully.

She shook her head, protesting. "Karen said it was
the fourth cabin. I counted."

The man beside her burst into laughter and her be-
wilderment turned to fury.

He saw her face redden, tried to stop laughing, and
the deep baritone rumble turned to a sputter as he
choked. With a terrific excuse for doing something she
wanted to do anyway, Jillian closed the yard and a half
between their chairs and thumped him wickedly between the shoulder blades with her fist.

He gasped. She raised her arm to repeat the treatment.

"No, you don't," he croaked, grabbing her wrist and pulling her down to the footstool in front of him. "I'll be okay in a minute."

She watched his struggle to draw air into his lungs and readied her fist.

"Did Karen tell Jim she was lending you the cabin?"

His question startled her. "You know Jim and Karen?"

He didn't need to nod. His expression said it all.

The pieces fell into place. "Jim lent *you* the cabin." She groaned, huddling toward the warmth of the fire, wrapping her arms around herself. "What a mess!"

"I'm willing to share if you are."

She gave him a sidelong look.

"It might be a little awkward when the boyfriend gets here, but we don't have to worry about that tonight."

"Why?"

"We can't go anywhere. And since the boyfriend isn't here yet, he's not coming."

"Oh, he'll be here."

He didn't say anything for a long moment, just ran a velvet gaze over her curves. His look seared everywhere it touched, and her breathing became shallow.

"I don't doubt he'll try." He spoke so softly that she had to lean closer to hear, "but he'll never make it unless he's driving a tank."

"You made it."

"Barely. Even though my Blazer has four-wheel drive, the last twenty miles took me more than an hour."

He stood up impatiently, jamming fingers into the pockets of his jeans. "You still haven't told me your name."

"Jillian Kemp."

"I guess we're roomies, Jillian Kemp." He smiled.

"At least till you can make other arrangements." Jillian wanted the matter straightened out now. The thought of having an observer during her week with Harrison sent cold chills down her spine. She'd talked Harrison out of going somewhere warm to *avoid* having an audience.

His answering chuckle wasn't encouraging. But surely he'd leave when the weather cleared.

The phone rang in the bedroom or she probably would have stared at him in dismay for the rest of the night.

"It's not for me," Matt said with a shrug. It rang again, sounding off-key in the primitive silence. "No one knows I'm here."

Jillian wondered whom he was hiding from as she made her way into the dark room and fumbled for the receiver. Karen was already talking by the time Jillian said hello.

"Oh, Jilly, you'll never guess what we've done! I thought I'd better call."

"It's okay, Karen. He's here."

Karen let out a long sigh, then laughed. "I'll bet you've got an interesting situation on your hands. Harrison must be fit to be tied."

"He probably would be," Jillian replied unhappily, "but he isn't here yet."

"Oh dear. That's not good."

"I know. He was supposed to be here around seven."

Karen didn't say anything.

Jillian asked hesitantly, "How's the weather there?"

"That's not good, either. The only way you can still get in or out of town is east on I-70. On the ten o'clock news, they were asking people to take in families who are stuck at the airport. Jim went out there a few minutes ago. I guess we're going to have company for Christmas, after all. I hope it's someone with kids. Then it won't be so bad not seeing my nieces and nephew."

"Karen." When Karen started working with her two years ago, Jillian had learned that when it was your turn to talk, you had to break in. "Will you call Harrison's folks and find out how long ago he left? Then call me back."

"Sure, hon."

"Your friend said he almost didn't make it."

"Matt said that? Then things *must* be bad. It really isn't such a terrible mix-up after all, Jilly. It's a good thing Matt's there. What do you think of him, anyway? Isn't he a hunk? He'll take care of you. Believe me, I wouldn't want to be alone at the lake in this blizzard. Which reminds me. Did you have any trouble with the propane? You found the breaker box? I'll bet things were a mess. It always takes me two days to clean up the place after it's been closed for a while."

"Everything's fine, except the—"

"Oh, you wanted me to call Harrison, didn't you?" Karen giggled. "Lordy, Jillian, you lucked out. Matt instead of Harrison? Oh, don't get all huffy," she rushed on when Jillian would have protested. "I know women who would kill to change places with you. But you'd better watch yourself. He's a heartbreaker."

"Oh? He said he came here because he wanted to be alone. Are you sure he isn't the one suffering?" Jillian instantly doubted her own intelligence. Karen had finally gasped for air and Jillian wasted her word-in-edgewise on something that didn't matter.

"Oh no, Jilly, I don't think so. He's just a loner. Jim asked him to spend Christmas with us, but he was hoping to get some work done. He insisted on going to the cabin. I hope he's not too upset by this. Apologize to him for us, will you?" She chuckled again. "And I'll apologize to Harrison the next time I see him. Especially if you use your time like I would if Jim wasn't such a sweetheart. Sometimes I'm tempted to join the chase for Matt myself. Which reminds me, I'm supposed to be finding out what's going on with Harrison, aren't I? I'll call you back in a minute." She hung up before Jillian could say goodbye.

The front door slammed and Jillian was suddenly terrified that Matt might have decided to leave her here, alone. She rushed to the other room as Matt came back in, his face ruddy from the bitter cold. His arms were loaded with brown paper bags.

"Hoping the boyfriend made it after all?" Matt asked as he passed her.

"Yes," she retorted, following him. She peeked into the bags he set on the counter.

"You'll be able to see better if you'll hold the flashlight while I unpack them."

She complied, watching as he tucked a head of lettuce under one elbow and took out a quart of milk and a couple of packages of fresh produce. When the refrigerator light didn't come on, she remembered. "Will everything be all right with the electricity off?"

"For the night anyway. If it's still off tomorrow, we'll do something else."

The door wouldn't close and he hunched down to rearrange things. "How about some light down here." He removed a jar of pickles and other assorted condiments and put them in the cabinet.

Even in a bulky coat—which looked straight from some thrift shop—he moved with an easy grace. It seemed at odds with the strength she'd felt when he embraced her.

"You must have brought enough to feed an army." He returned her attention to the groceries.

"We—Harrison and I—are staying until New Year's," she explained.

"Me, too." His back was toward hers but she heard his grin.

"We'll see."

"I guess we will," he agreed as the phone rang again.

Plopping the flashlight on the counter, she ran for the other room.

"Jillian? I'm not going to make it tonight." Harrison's voice competed with static as he answered her greeting. "I'm..." A crackle buried the rest of his sentence.

"Are you all right? Where are you?"

"I'm fine," he reassured her loudly. "I'm still at the office. Mom called a minute ago and said I was supposed to call Karen. She gave me the number there. I'm sorry you were worried."

A shadow blocked the little bit of light feathering into the room. Jillian glanced at the figure by the door. Despite the silence, she lodged a finger against her free ear and turned to face the wall.

"Are you there?" Harrison shouted.

"Yes," she answered softly.

"What?"

"Yes. I'm sorry, Harrison. I missed what you just said." She sensed Matt moving closer.

"I asked if everything was okay? Are you snowed in?"

"I'm fine. I haven't been out since I got here this afternoon, but it looks pretty bad." Matt nudged her, then pushed the flashlight into her hand and left. She breathed easier.

"You're going to have to speak up, darling," Harrison said.

She repeated her last sentence, then bit the corner of her lip. Why hadn't she told him about her "visitor"?

His voice deepened with meaning. "I'll be with you as soon as I can, darling—as soon as the highways are open."

"You can't control the weather," she said, excusing him. "What happened?"

"You know how things are. The unofficial office party got under way about two this afternoon, and just when I was ready to go all the senior partners showed up. By the time I could leave diplomatically, they'd closed the airport and were starting on the highways. It would have been foolhardy to try making it all the way out there, so I stayed here."

Jillian squelched a twinge of resentment.

"I think I've made a few inroads with one of the partners," Harrison said excitedly. "That should help secure our future. It may not be as long as I figured before I'm offered a partnership."

"Well, I'm sure your mother will be delighted to have you home after all," she said stiffly.

"I can't imagine why. I've gone skiing every Christmas since my junior year in high school."

"Your mother thinks you were going skiing?"

"She assumed that. I didn't enlighten her."

You wouldn't have told Grandma these plans, she defended him to herself. *You wouldn't be* here *if Grandma was alive,* a tiny voice answered back.

"I wouldn't miss our time together for anything, Jillian. I'll be there as soon as I can."

"Maybe it's just as well you didn't make it tonight." She tried to sound cheerful. "Things aren't at all like we planned. The electricity is off." She gulped and plunged ahead. "And did Karen tell you about the mix-up?" She played nervously with the telephone cord. "At least I'm not totally alone," she added when he didn't answer.

"Harrison?" The line was strangely silent after all the static. "Harrison?" She clicked the switch hook and heard absolutely nothing. Sitting with a dead phone to her ear, she felt a confusing mixture of relief, annoyance and guilt.

When had the line gone dead? Had he heard about the electricity? And why the hesitation to tell him about Matt? He surely wouldn't worry as much if he knew she wasn't alone. She had to get over this reluctance to share things with Harrison. At least *he* could call Karen if he wanted the details, she thought irritably. *She* couldn't do anything about her situation.

Harrison can't control the weather, her reasonable side explained to her uncharitable self. He'd been trying to get her to go away with him since they met.

So why wasn't he here? Jillian couldn't help feeling a little betrayed. If he'd left when he was supposed to, he would have arrived before the weather got so bad.

Then she'd have him *and* Matt to deal with!

If Harrison were here, Matt's arrival wouldn't have been any big deal. She wouldn't have felt threatened. She wouldn't have assumed he was Harrison. She wouldn't have kissed him. That kiss... It had felt right, and wonderful...and...

It didn't make sense.

Maybe all those desires she'd held in check for so long had surfaced with a vengeance once she decided to come out of the Dark Ages. For the past month she'd been watching romantic movies, reading sexy books and trying to make sure she was "normal." Harrison wasn't the first man who'd suggested she might be frigid. She hadn't wanted him to get here and be convinced he was right.

She looked down at the silent receiver she still held and hung it up. The wind howled through the tree branches outside. Jillian shivered and went to look. Snow swirled madly. Ice crystals decorated one pane of the quartered window. She pressed a cheek against the cold surface and let it soothe her.

"I wish you were here, Grandma. You could always make sense out of everything." Then she smiled wryly. The last person she would want here was Grandma. She'd have a fit!

"I still wish you were here," she murmured to the frozen landscape outside. Her breath fogged the view. It reminded her that she should go and find out what Matt was up to. She refused to let him make her feel like a drop of water skipping across a hot griddle.

She closed her eyes to think of Harrison, but it was Matt's image that popped into focus. Try as she might, she couldn't seem to replace his face with Harrison's patrician features. It didn't matter, she decided. Matt, the blizzard and getting through the next couple of days were her main worries, and until the outside world became a reality again, there wasn't any point in thinking about it.

Matt had brought in more wood, she noticed as she came through the living room. He was pulling food out of the freezer compartment when Jillian returned to the kitchen. "Want to hold the flashlight again?" he asked.

She positioned herself beside him and aimed the light on the box.

"I take it the call was from the boyfriend."

"I wish you wouldn't say 'the boyfriend' like that."

"Like what?" He put the last package of meat in the box.

She looked at the dark hands splayed across the top of the frozen packages, aware that she was being critical of Harrison right now and probably attributing her own feelings to Matt's innocent remarks. She changed the subject. "Why aren't you spending Christmas with your family?"

He lifted one shoulder and placed the ice cube trays on the frozen meat. "My mother just left for Europe with her fourth 'new' husband. And my sister wanted me to join her family, but I didn't think I could take her ever-hopeful parade of 'eligible' women, so I used her houseful of in-laws as an excuse and escaped here."

"What about friends?" He looked like a man any number of women would be delighted to have grace their festivities. She could name at least three of *her* friends who would include him after one glance.

"This is fine." His low chuckle spread to his eyes, making them spark wildly. "My sister would love this setup. An isolated cabin, a snowstorm and a beautiful elf from Santa." He'd stopped folding in the flaps of the cardboard box. "I can think of worse ways to spend the holidays."

Her eyes widened and the pace of her heart picked up.

"Of course, her version would be a bit more romantic than mine. She'd have us married off on New Year's Day."

"And your version?" The words slipped out before Jillian could stop them, and she held her breath.

"My version would never work. I don't think you're the type." He pushed back a strand of her fine, almost gossamer, hair. "You don't look the type to schedule this kind of rendezvous with your boyfriend either, though."

She flushed.

"You look as innocent as Sleeping Beauty." He fingered the white lace-edged collar of her jumpsuit; the back of his hand grazed the underside of her chin. "Maybe I should play the handsome prince."

Her hand loosened on the flashlight. It clattered to the floor and went out. They both bent for it and almost bumped heads. He grasped her shoulder, steadying her, but released her immediately. The imprint of his hand seemed to remain.

Matt fiddled with the light, switched it back on and returned it to her with a look that warned her to hang on to it this time.

"What are you going to do with that?" she asked to ease the tension as he finished closing the forgotten box.

"We'll set it outside."

"What about wild animals?"

"Which wild animals do you mean?" She heard his amusement as he carried the box to the door.

She shrugged. "I don't know."

He came back and grabbed another, smaller box. "Here. I'll hold the box and you can load the rest of the frozen food into it. Okay?"

They were finished in a minute and he took both cartons outside.

"Cold, huh?" he said as he came in and grasped her face between his hands.

She shivered and returned the favor. "Mine, too. That was *frozen* food."

"Which is what will keep scavengers away. No scent to attract them."

His mustache twitched beneath her thumb, making her skin tingle. A muscle tightened in his scruffy jaw. Warmth emanated from him and she laughed nervously, embarrassed at how long she'd caressed his face. "Your warm skin feels nice on my cold hands."

"Warm heart?" he murmured, covering her hands with his as she started to draw them away. His lips parted. Weakness seeped into her knees and she sagged a bit. She suddenly wanted him to kiss her again. She swallowed, her heart ticking like a metronome set on allegro.

"Do you know what you're doing?" he asked quietly, his face moving a smidgen closer, his gaze lingering on her mouth.

Her heavy eyelids flew open. He *knew* she wanted him to kiss her.

"Are you inviting me to step in for the boyfriend?"

She snatched her hands back, clasping them in front of her. "Are you nuts?" She knew her face betrayed her.

"Then don't start anything you don't want to finish," he warned mildly, thrusting his fingers into the pockets of his already tight jeans.

Needing something to do, she grabbed the flashlight from the counter and hurried into the other room to collect their mugs. He hadn't moved when she returned.

She gestured toward him with what was left of the wine, offering him the remainder. He refused with a shake of his head, and she poured the rest of it down the sink.

"That first call was from Karen," she said to break the lengthening silence. "They'd just discovered the mix-up. Karen is glad you're here. I don't believe she thinks I'd know what to do in a blizzard."

"Would you?" She kept her eyes on the bubbles multiplying in the sink while she ran a couple of inches of dishwater. He propped himself on the counter and watched.

"I'd manage."

"Why aren't *you* with your family?" Matt asked.

She didn't answer immediately, then... "Do you believe in guardian angels?"

He looked at her as if her biscuits weren't quite baked, to use a favorite expression of her grandmother's, and she smiled.

"I was thinking of my grandmother. She sent you here so I wouldn't be alone."

"I don't know your grandmother."

He was really looking at her strangely now. "She died in August. Otherwise, I'd be with her for the holidays."

His face relaxed as he caught on. "What about the rest of your family?"

"My mother and father died when I was small. Grandma raised me." She pulled the plug and let the water gurgle down the drain.

"No one else?"

She shook her head. "I was an only child. So were my folks. I guess that's why I've always wanted lots of kids when I get married. Grandma was wonderful, but I was always a little lonely."

"Okay. So Grandma's playing guardian angel. Why did she send me? Why not the boyfriend?"

Jillian was facing him now and she blushed.

"She wouldn't have approved of my plans with Harrison," she admitted. "But she wouldn't have wanted me to be totally alone, either."

From his amused look, she was afraid he understood more than she wanted him to.

What would Grandma think of Matt? she wondered.

She'd have liked him a lot. Jillian didn't even need to consider it. Instead of showing him her marble-topped table that came west in a covered wagon and making small talk, as she had the first time she met Harrison, Grandma and Matt would have cozied up to the kitchen table, eating pie and talking like long-lost buddies in their matter-of-fact, first-things-first language.

"So what do we do now?"

She wrinkled her brow at the mischievous twinkle in his eye.

"When Harry gets here," he said in answer to her questioning frown. "If Grandma sent me to play gooseberry, what am I supposed to do? I'd be shirking my responsibilities if I left."

Jillian's mouth dropped open. "That's just the word she would have used."

Matt smiled and Jillian knew, just knew, that she was in trouble if he took her ramblings seriously. She didn't think she could stand to be "protected" from herself—not by him, anyway.

She turned away and started toward the bedroom. "The stress is beginning to get to me. I think it's time for bed."

Matt followed. "If you'll just let me get some blankets out of the closet in there, I'll take the couch. It converts into a bed." She stopped outside the bedroom door.

He emerged as she finished casting aside the cushions. Together, they pulled out the couch and he fluttered one of the sheets out over the mattress. They worked silently until the bed was made.

"Well, I've had all I can take for one day. I'll see you in the morning." She paused again at the door of the bedroom.

"I'm sorry the boyfriend didn't make it." He sounded sincere.

She smiled wryly. "And I've messed up your plans for a quiet Christmas."

Matt started toward her and she backed two steps into the other room.

"You'd better have the flashlight." He passed it to her. She felt ridiculous. "Good night," she murmured, then changed her mind and rejoined him at the door. "I'm glad you're here, Matt Carson. I couldn't have handled this holiday alone."

"I know, Jillian Kemp. Good night."

As she closed the door behind her, he raised his voice to add, "Merry Christmas . . . Jake."

CHAPTER THREE

JILLIAN USUALLY NEEDED at least three nudges from the alarm clock before she could get her eyes open, but on Christmas morning she woke before daylight. She reached over to the nightstand for her watch, and understood immediately what had jarred her awake. It was *freezing* in the room. She yanked the covers tight as her breath rose like a cloud around her face.

Moments later, she decided it wasn't going to get any warmer where she was and bravely slipped her feet out from under the blanket. Her usually warm slippers felt like ice.

Pulling the top quilt over her, she grabbed her robe and headed, shivering, for the other room, praying she'd find heat there.

As soon as she opened the bedroom door, warmth seeped in around the folds of the blanket. The closer she got to the fire, the warmer it was, and she scowled at the sight of her roomie.

Mr. Snug-as-a-bug Matt Carson had a bare arm sprawled across his pillow. His one blanket covered him only to the waist. At least he could have kept the fire going, she thought disgustedly, eyeing the few sad-looking lumps of glowing wood.

She dropped her quilt just long enough to put on her robe. Flinging a couple of logs into the fireplace, she poked about as if she knew what she was doing, then rewrapped herself. She sat down on the hearth.

Matt hadn't moved. His ashy-blond hair stuck up at odd angles, his full lower lip curved into a half smile. She fumed. His broad shoulders were bare to the warmth, and his free-form flop indicated how comfortably *he'd* spent the night.

Her own bones ached from shivering and she fought the urge to yank the covers off him. She cleared her throat loudly and had the satisfaction of seeing him move. One leg slithered out from beneath its hiding place and his foot curled around the edge of his blanket. She stemmed her irritation by remembering that this was Christmas, after all. And she didn't relish spending another holiday in solitary misery.

She glanced at the fire as the logs she'd added sputtered noisily. Harrison would have been as helpless in this situation as she felt. If they hadn't frozen to death first, they would have let all the meat thaw and then have decided to put it outside in nature's refrigerator. The animals would have appreciated their ineptitude.

Considering the situation, the golden man framed in the expanse of white sheets was a big bonus.

But why was he here? She studied him. He had family. Why would you avoid your family during the holidays?

For that matter, why had Harrison planned to come? He'd suggested spending Christmas together when he saw how upset she was after Thanksgiving. She'd eagerly agreed, assuming he was inviting her to share Christmas with his family.

"Lord, no," he said, "I wouldn't inflict them on anyone. We'll have plenty of time for family obligations after we're married. You'll have the rest of your life to put up with them.''

"But since we're announcing our engagement—''

He'd stopped her in midsentence by kissing her. "I want you to myself. I need you so much, Jillian. You'd feel the same way if you'd only let go." He'd kissed her again, coaxing her, sensing her hesitation. "We could go somewhere warm. St. Croix, maybe?"

"No." He frowned until she explained. "Please, let's go somewhere personal, private. I don't think I could handle hordes of people. Besides, I want our first Christmas together to be traditional." She'd told him about Karen's cabin—remaining wistfully silent about her desire to meet his family.

Harrison was the youngest of four children. His siblings were all married with children of their own. A house *filled* with people you loved? Not to spend Christmas with them?

Men! She'd never figure them out. What she wouldn't give for even one more day with Grandma. She sniffed once and dabbed the corner of her eye with the quilt.

Heat drifted toward her in waves. She moved to one of the wing-back chairs and tucked her feet under her, feeling drowsy.

She couldn't get comfortable.

Matt's bed drew her, seduced her, until she gave in, crawled onto the corner of the lumpy mattress and curled into a tight ball.

She wouldn't go to sleep, but maybe, if she just used the very edge of the bed, the one closest to the fire, she could rest a bit. After the moment of temporary insanity last night, when she'd wanted him to kiss her, she hated to think what he'd assume if he found her in his bed.

Matt turned over and she lunged away.

Rising to her knees, she peered past the arm draped over his head. His eyes were still closed. His light brown lashes, tipped with gold, seemed bright against his tan. He looked innocent, like a little boy. All he needed to do to dispel that impression was open those wise, knowing eyes.

He turned again, tugging the blanket with him as he went, wrapping it into a mummy-tight shroud. She blushed, realizing that the blanket was his only covering. At his sigh, her gaze jerked to his face. The sigh became a miniature snore, and she exhaled slowly, then resumed her position on the other side of the bed. She relaxed cautiously, willing her short nervous breaths to even out, then closed her eyes to rest them from the smoky heat.

"THIS IS GETTING better and better." Matt's face filled her view as her eyes popped open. Sunlight streamed in the window, framing his head like a halo. He was dressed but lying beside her, his head propped up on his fist. "Did you change your mind about me stepping in for Harry?" he asked, any resemblance to an angel vanishing instantly.

"The heat is off in the bedroom," she said, drawing back to put some distance between them.

His white teeth brightened his freshly shaved face. "I know," he admitted, and amusement brimmed in his eyes. "I'd decided you couldn't resist me, then went in to get dressed and found out the truth. It was such a disappointment." He tried to look crushed but didn't manage it.

She sat up self-consciously and attempted to smooth her wildly disarrayed hair.

"You look like a wide-eyed Sleeping Beauty," he said, "even more than you did last night. As long as you keep looking that way I have half a chance of convincing myself to keep my hands off you."

Bunching the quilt around her, Jillian blinked rapidly, trying to get her eyes to focus so she could think. The way he was looking at her made it difficult to do anything but listen to her heart pound.

"It's not going to be easy." He cleared his throat and stood up. Walking to the fireplace, he removed the thumbtack from the hand-knitted stocking she'd hung beside the matching, more masculine one for Harrison. "Santa has been here." The stocking landed in her lap before she could react.

"But that's impossible."

He laughed. "Haven't you been a good little girl?"

She lifted the quilted patchwork stocking gingerly. The "something" in it was an almost imperceptible lump in the toe. She looked up at him, stunned. "But how could you—"

"Do I look like Santa? He must have sneaked in sometime between when we went to bed and when you crawled in with me."

She tipped the sock, watching delightedly as a slender silver chain flowed into her hand.

"Go on," he urged.

She tugged gently. An enameled sprig of holly connected two silver bells to the necklace. Tiny silver chains with diamonds at their tips represented strikers. "It's beautiful." Her eyes hadn't left it. Reluctantly she pushed the necklace toward him. "But I can't accept it." Somehow, she'd moved to the end of the bed and was kneeling across from where he sat in the chair.

He pushed her arm back. "I don't see why not."

"You didn't know I'd be here. How did you . . . where did you get it?"

She looked from the bells to him. His flannel plaid shirt bore signs of many washings, the pocket edges frayed. The necklace wasn't excessively expensive, but it wasn't cheap, either. The bells were obviously handcrafted by a skilled metalsmith. He'd had this specially made for someone.

"Ohh, I see," she whispered sympathetically. No wonder he was here. He was hiding out. He and the woman had quarreled; they'd—

"There's nothing to see. Don't go inventing star-crossed lovers or anything. I happen to sell jewelry. I had a few samples in the Blazer. A friend of mine made that and I wanted to give you something unique." He let out a deep breath. "You're making me regret my impulse."

"It was a very sweet impulse." He winced at the word *sweet*. "I think you should give it to your mother or sister or someone special." She held it out again.

This time, he took it. Rising from his chair, he sat down beside her on the bed. "Don't worry. They all got something." He turned her by the shoulders until her back was toward him. "I'm giving this to you." He put it around her neck, fumbling with the clasp for a time before uttering an expletive. "Could you hold this out of the way?"

She lifted her wild hair. His fingers tickled her neck, sending silky, shivery waves down her spine.

"There aren't any strings attached?" she asked quietly, almost afraid to hear the answer.

"Dammit." Grasping her a little more firmly this time, he turned her to face him again. "This is the first thing I've done on impulse in years. I caught a belated touch of Christmas spirit because, for once, I had the chance to give something that wasn't expected. And you ask about strings. That's almost funny." He hesitated, searching her eyes with his, then briefly tasted her surprised lips. "That's it," he assured her, "the only obligation. I've just collected." He moved quickly to the pile of logs beside the fire and put another one on top of the still-blazing stack in the fireplace.

"You're a very nice man," she said, fingering the warm chain where it rested on the back of her neck. "Thank you. I'm sorry I suspected your motives."

He shrugged, gazing at the fire until the log crackled and settled noisily into the flames. When he finally looked her way again, the uncharacteristic sternness had left his face.

Then she remembered the giving. Christmas was giving.

He eyed her sudden frown warily.

When she joined him and reached for the other stocking, Matt stilled her hand. "No."

"I can't accept your gift then," she told him soberly, her hands going to the clasp of the necklace. "This was a lovely thought. I wish I'd had it first."

"But you picked that out for—"

"Harrison won't miss one little gift. He'll still have those." She indicated the brightly wrapped packages under the tree.

Matt agreed reluctantly.

"I didn't pick this out for Harrison anyway," Jillian admitted, pushing the stocking at him. She watched the small bottle fall into his hand. "I picked it out because it's my favorite cologne. It's just a small gift."

Matt thanked her warmly. Jillian thought about returning his kiss and decided against it. She was feeling much too emotional. It suddenly *felt* like Christmas. Her throat hurt. She was afraid she'd cry. She swallowed hard to get rid of the lump in her throat. "We cheated, you know."

He raised an eyebrow.

"Grandma would never let me open my gifts until we had breakfast. I made her traditional specialty— Swedish tea ring. Would you like some?"

His nod was his biggest movement since she'd given him Harrison's stocking. Maybe, for once, she'd left *him* speechless. She smiled and excused herself to heat the braided bread ring she'd decorated with cherries and nuts. Matt had already made coffee.

When he joined her a few minutes later, she accepted his offer of help by asking him to set the table. As he passed her, carrying the dishes, she got a whiff of the cologne she'd given him and felt disproportionately happy.

"Do you think they'll manage to clear the roads today?" Jillian asked much later as they finished their second meal of the day. The table groaned under the weight of their Christmas feast, and Matt, still eating, shook his head and shrugged. From her vantage point by the window, Jillian looked out at the sun-washed landscape and illogically hoped they wouldn't.

Ice glazed every tree, shrub and weed between the porch and the lake. And with the snow, everything glimmered like diamonds. Leaning farther back, she tried to catch a glimpse of the road. A drift, running from the corner of the cabin roof to where she guessed the road began, obscured her vision. "The snow always looks so pristine after a storm—I hate when they ruin it."

Matt pushed himself away from the table. "Don't worry, we aren't going to be high on anyone's list," he said, dabbing his mouth with her grandmother's holly-patterned napkin.

"Because we're so far from the highway?"

"Partly," he nodded. "They may not even mess with us after Christmas. These are mostly summer vacation cottages. They may not realize anyone's stuck down here."

"I hope that doesn't mean they won't fix the electricity."

"Probably depends on where it's out. It'll cost triple-time to have anyone working on Christmas Day, and if the line's down between here and the main road, the power company may not even know. No one else may be affected." He leaned back, tipping his chair up on two legs.

Jillian watched the chair lurch precariously and resisted the urge to ask if he was trying to kill himself. He'd probably resent anyone fussing over him.

How little she knew about him. He continually surprised and fascinated her, but she still didn't *know* anything about him.

Although he'd avoided his family over Christmas and said he wanted to be alone, he'd teased her, talking and acting as if he enjoyed her company. And he obviously didn't mind work, because he'd willingly shared the preparations for Christmas dinner. His culinary skills had contributed the wonderful cornbread-and-oyster stuffing—a traditional "must," he'd said.

She suspected that his see-straight-into-your-soul gaze had identified her capable side. Her fair hair, heart-shaped face and large blue eyes, packaged with her miniature, not quite five-foot frame, had always masked a tough determination. One that few people recognized.

Grandma had worked hard at teaching her to take care of herself. She'd treated her like someone who could share the load—just as Matt did. And he'd eaten two pieces of the mincemeat pie she'd made from Grandma's recipe. Two! Even though it lacked Grandma's tender touch. Jillian sighed.

Matt scowled, emphasizing the permanent wrinkle between his brows. "What's the matter?" he asked.

"I was thinking of Grandma."

"You miss her a lot, don't you?"

She nodded. "She spoiled me rotten. Not with things—she couldn't afford to spoil me that way—but she gave me so much love."

Matt leaned forward, resting his chin on his fist.

His interest unnerved her. Jillian noticed the empty coffee mugs and went to get the pot. "Would you like more coffee?" she asked from the kitchen.

He held out his cup as she reappeared.

"It's nice to talk about her without..." She shrugged and set the almost empty pot on the table.

"Maybe it's easier because I don't know you."

"Maybe, but I hope it's because I'm finally adjusting to her death." She stared into the fire. "She made school vacations so special. We'd bake and decorate, put puzzles together, eat popcorn. In the evenings she'd read tear-jerkers aloud. Classics like *A Tale of Two Cities*. We'd both cry."

Matt laid a hand on top of hers, and she looked over at him and sniffed.

"I'd better not get started. You'll drown." She smiled tremulously. "She could never afford to give me what I really wanted for Christmas. Not anything as lovely as this." Her fingers lightly stroked the chain he'd given her. "But what she gave, she gave with so much love it didn't matter." This time when she looked at him, her eyes did fill with tears.

"I'm sorry." She forced the words from her tight throat.

He stood up, came around the table and held out his arms. They folded around her as she buried her face against the soft fabric covering his shoulder, muffling her quiet sobs. He stroked her hair, murmuring comforting words.

She felt Matt's strength ebbing into her. With a final noisy sniff, she drew back, immediately missing his warmth. He moved away. Swiping at the remaining tears with a knuckle, she gratefully accepted the tissue he extended as he returned.

"Thank you." It bothered Harrison when she cried. The one time she'd let go, shortly after the funeral, he'd acted as though a monster had backed him into a corner. "I'm sorry, but I miss her so much." She needed to say it to someone and Matt seemed willing to listen. "Sometimes I feel so alone."

"You're not alone. I'm here." His voice was soothing.

"You know what I mean." She raised her face toward his.

He pulled her close, cupping her chin in his hand. "I'll help you remember you're not alone." His head descended a fraction. "My body keeps reminding me," he murmured ruefully.

Her breath caught. Her red-rimmed eyes widened, then fluttered closed as his lips edged nearer. Her heartbeat quickened as he sighed against her lips.

His kiss branded her with its gentleness. Her hand drifted to the back of his head—to coax him closer. The tip of his tongue searched her mouth tentatively, seeking more; her lips parted, encouraging him.

He lifted his head, slowly dislodging her hand from its tight hold on his neck.

"This is insanity," he whispered, his eyes never leaving her lips. His arm still molded her to his body. "I'm not sure who's crazier. Me, for not taking what's offered, or you, for offering yourself because you need to be close to someone right now." With a derisive laugh, he stepped away from her.

Her common sense returned with a jolt. She could thank her lucky stars that he'd recognized her confusion and hadn't taken advantage of that desperate blend of emotional need and physical longing. A minute ago, she would have gone along with anything he asked.

"I have one rule that's served me well. Anything that happens between intelligent, consenting adults is fair," he said. "But this situation is too emotional to fall into that category." He rubbed his neck, looking at her for the first time since he'd backed away. "Whether you know it or not, you are a very seductive witch, and I don't know how long I can take all this togetherness. Let's get out of here. How about a walk?"

She eyed the heavily laden table, then gazed out the window. The sun had been inviting her all day, even though she knew it was cold out. And thanks to that kiss, she could definitely use a cooling off. "Okay. We'd better clear the table first."

He reluctantly picked up the relish plate and followed her to the kitchen. When they'd collected all the dishes and she began running hot water, he reached past her to turn off the tap. "It's time," he said. "The table is clean."

"Shouldn't we put away the food?"

He shook his head. "By now, it'll stay as cool sitting out on the counter as it would be in the fridge." He looked thoughtful. "We'll have to do something about that when we get back."

"What will we do if they don't fix the electricity soon?" Jillian asked.

"We'll stay warm enough with the fire going, and we can leave the oven on if we need to. We certainly won't run out of food. But it wouldn't hurt to call the power company when we come back. They can't fix it if they don't know it's out."

Jillian grimaced. "The phone's out, too." She'd forgotten to tell him.

"Well, that explains why the boyfriend hasn't called to wish you Merry Christmas." Matt lifted a shoulder. "I, myself, won't miss it. Let's get out of here."

"Do I need more than a coat?"

"What are the choices?"

"I brought long johns."

"Good! I'll put mine on, too, and we can stay out longer." He followed her into the bedroom, searching for his pair in the suitcase he'd left open in the corner.

She fidgeted as she watched him churn through his belongings. Pulling out her own underwear with him in the room seemed too intimate an act to contemplate. "I'll wait till you're finished," she muttered, and went to the door.

"I'll change in the bathroom," he offered.

"No, that's okay." She closed the door behind her.

"Meet me outside," he told her as they exchanged places a few minutes later.

Jillian hurried and was soon cramming her pale gold hair under a vivid red cap and letting herself out the back door.

Expecting Matt to be waiting impatiently, Jillian frowned when she didn't see him. She wandered to the side of the cabin and looked toward the lake. A loosely packed snowball caught her unexpectedly as she turned the corner. She whirled as Matt emerged from behind a tree, but decided not to retaliate. It didn't seem worth the effort—not when he was expecting it. Maybe later.

"Very funny," she said with an exaggerated smile.

"I couldn't resist." Matt approached her cautiously, obviously surprised at her casual response to the snowball.

He looked sleek and powerful in his black body-hugging ski suit. He was carrying something long and narrow—skis? she wondered.

"I got my bow out of the Blazer."

"I guess I'm lucky it was just a snowball that hit me." She eyed the arrows attached to the side of the bow.

"Maybe I'll get tomorrow's lunch."

"What are you planning?" she asked, not sure she wanted to know.

"We may scare up a rabbit or two."

"Ugh." She shuddered as he skirted the side of the cabin and led her toward the thickest stand of trees.

He climbed to the top of a four-foot drift, extending a hand down to her. "Be careful. Everything's icy."

She accepted his help and held on to him till they were over the ridge. "I wore my waffle-stompers," she commented, indicating her footprint pattern in the crisp snow.

"Ugh." He imitated her earlier shudder as he looked at her hiking boots. "Remind me to eat out when you fix waffles, Jake."

"Why do you keep calling me that?"

"It's shorter than Jillian Kemp."

Suddenly, she felt invigorated, light as the cotton-ball clouds that floated in the dazzlingly bright sky, looking close enough to touch. She inhaled deeply.

"Tell me about Harry," Matt said conversationally.

Startled at the mention of the man who had hardly entered her mind all day, she didn't answer.

"What's he do?" Matt turned back to look at her, not losing a step.

"He's a lawyer," she answered, then added with emphasis, "his name's Harrison."

"And you're engaged to him?"

He flung the question over his shoulder indifferently, but she'd noticed him studying her hand during lunch and gladly clarified the situation. "Informally. I'm getting the ring for Christmas."

He was silent and she assumed he found the subject as unappealing as she suddenly did. Discussing Harrison usually seemed exciting. Discussing Harrison with Matt seemed like a betrayal.

"Where'd you meet him?" he asked finally, helping her over a small snowdrift.

"At a barbecue for my boss."

He gave her a look that invited her to expand on her answer.

"I work for a senator."

"Oh? Which one?"

"Mike Atwater."

"He's okay," he responded, surprising her as she prepared for all the standard political gripes she usually received when people learned about her job.

"So where did Harry come in?"

"Harrison," she corrected again. "The barbecue was a fund-raiser during the last campaign."

"That was more than a year ago. Harry's not a very decisive character, is he?"

"We didn't start seeing each other right away."

"Not exactly love at first sight, huh?"

She shot a warning look at his back. "I've always thought the kind of love that lasts is built on friendship and mutual respect."

"I wouldn't know, but it sounds boring as heck."

"As long as we're getting personal, how about you? Are you married, divor—"

"Single."

"Never been married?"

His "no" was emphatic. "I have a perfectly healthy regard for your sex. Why would I want to ruin it?"

They tramped silently for a while. As they moved deeper into the trees, the ground leveled off. The wind hadn't piled all the snow in heaps here. Matt picked up his pace and Jillian practically had to jog to keep up.

"Do you hunt a lot?" she panted, breaking their silence.

He slowed down. "When I get the chance. Dad and I used to go off almost every weekend."

"Really? You haven't mentioned your father before. Where is he?"

"Heaven, I hope. Or some equivalent."

"Oh. I'm sorry."

"He died when I was seventeen. I've had lots of time to get used to it." His voice held more affection for his father than it had when he'd spoken of his sister and mother.

"How old are you now?" she asked, wondering how long it took to "get used to" a loved one's death.

"Thirty-one. It's been fourteen years," he replied, sparing her the calculation.

"Maybe that's why your mother's been married so many times."

Matt stopped so suddenly, she ran into him. "I don't see the connection." He turned to face her, scowling.

"Well...you didn't sound like you approved of your mother's fourth marriage. Has it ever occurred to you that maybe she can't get used to being without your father? Maybe she keeps remarrying to find what she had with him."

His laughter filled the stillness and a couple of birds took flight, setting ice-laden branches clattering like wooden wind chimes.

"Hardly. My mother and father couldn't stand each other. I never figured out how they got tangled up in the first place, let alone had two kids. They divorced when I was nine. They should have done it sooner."

"Oh. You were separated from your father several years before he died?"

"No. I stayed with him. Maureen, my sister, went with Mom."

"Oh," she repeated.

"Oh," he mimicked, brushing a low branch and showering her with ice as he set off down a makeshift path between the trees. "What wonderful insight do you think you've gained now?"

"I can see how watching your parents' marriage disintegrate might make you a little leery."

He laughed again. "Watching anyone's marriage might make me leery. Think about it. How many couples do you know who'd do it all over again if they could turn back the clock?"

"Lots of them."

"Name names."

"Well . . ." It irked her that she couldn't rattle off a list. His arrogance as he strolled leisurely away made her indignant.

"There's one of my neighbors. She's been married almost thirty years," she called breathlessly, rushing to catch up. "Her husband sends her flowers out of the blue, and for their anniversary last spring, he took her to Excelsior Springs. They had a very romantic second honeymoon in the spas."

"That's one," he acknowledged, stomping along with his head down.

"One of my friends from high school got married right after we graduated. She's so happy with her husband and their new baby that it's contagious. I feel happy just being with her."

He stopped. "But is her husband?" His cynical tone earned him a scathing look.

"How about Jim and Karen? We both know them. Don't you think they're happy?"

"Yes, but they each make their own happiness! Karen doesn't rely on Jim to fulfill her or vice versa. Now think of the ones you know who *aren't* happy," he challenged silkily.

"No!"

He raised an eyebrow derisively. She sank onto a large, ice-frosted rock, then found herself starting to slide. Grabbing her, he held her in place until she regained her balance, then released her and continued speaking. "Can't count 'em, can you?"

"I refuse to be a...a..."

"Happy pessimist?" he finished for her. "Like me?" He sat down in the snow, his back against a tree.

"What about kids? Would you rather your parents didn't have you?"

He chuckled. "The imminent birth of my sister is what got them into the mess in the first place. But you're right. If I wanted a family, I'd want to be married. Guess I've never had the itch for kids *or* a wife."

"Seriously, I don't know that many people who are unhappy with their marriages," Jillian told him.

"No," he agreed, surprising her, "but most people aren't happy, either. They're indifferent." He leaned forward. "You don't have to convince me. Some people just aren't cut out for it."

"You, for instance?"

He nodded. "And my dad. He was one terrific father when he was around, but a lousy husband. After they split up, Mom and Dad both turned into nice people. Mom's the type who should be married—she proves it by switching husbands frequently, just so no one gets left out—and Dad needed to stop by the pool hall after work with no one yelling about supper getting cold when he came home. I didn't blame my mother for leaving him. She needed to feel her life was going someplace. He was content with having nothing and living on past glories."

Jillian sighed. It all sounded so sad.

"And you believe in happily-ever-after?" There was a trace of condescension in his voice.

She nodded, trying to ignore a sudden feeling of unease.

"For your sake, I hope it exists."

"I know it does," she said fervently. She tried to think the pleasant thoughts about her future with Harrison that usually made her feel so satisfied.

"Don't you have any dreams or ambitions? Most of the women I know have big career plans. Eventually, they want a kid or two, but they make it sound like a hobby on the side."

Jillian's laugh gurgled up. Most of her friends were the same way. Even Lisa, her friend from high school, attended classes at Emporia State and planned to have a nursing degree by the time her children were in school.

"I'm a throwback, I guess. Karen calls me a dinosaur. *She's* going to law school as well as working. I'll miss her when she graduates next year. She tries to talk me into going back to school, but I can't think of anything I really want to do."

"Maybe you need more time. You shouldn't rush into marriage just to have something to do."

"That's not it at all. The only thing I've *ever* wanted to be—other than a wife and mother—was a concert pianist. It didn't take me too long to figure out that it would involve loads of work and a lot of travel. I'd have to give up having any kind of family life. I couldn't face that idea." She grimaced. "I do plan to give piano lessons after Harrison and I start a family of our own."

"You could teach music at school."

She wrinkled her nose. "That sounds appalling. See what I mean?"

"What about money? A lot of women have to work these days."

"We'll be in good shape. Harrison joined his father's old law firm as soon as he passed the bar exam, so he's not exactly struggling to establish a practice." His warm eyes felt cold on her now, and his eyebrow was raised. "If you think I'm marrying Harrison because he has money, you're wrong. But I am very practical. I'm delighted that I fell in love with someone who could afford my dreams. I want time to raise my kids. I don't want them trudging off to school in thrift shop clothing. I want to give them things I never had." She added defensively, "And I don't see the difference between wanting to marry well and being ambitious. If a man isn't ambitious, he's considered a failure."

"Like my father," Matt commented absently. "What would have happened if you fell in love with a poor man?"

"Luckily, I—"

Matt raised a gloved hand, motioning her not to speak. Her eyes followed his to the edge of the clearing. A rabbit sat there, partially camouflaged beneath a shrub.

Matt pulled off his glove with his teeth and slowly dropped into a crouch, threading an arrow onto the string of his bow.

She unconsciously put a hand on his arm.

His quizzical cat's eyes met hers across the arc of the bow as he drew it back to his cheek.

"Don't," she whispered, realizing she could have shouted and frightened the paralyzed animal away. "Please?"

He hesitated.

"We've got enough food to last us, don't we?"

He nodded and loosened his hold a bit.

"I couldn't eat him," she mouthed.

He debated, then lowered the weapon.

The rabbit scurried off at the sudden movement, quickly blending with the snow and undergrowth.

"Thank you."

Matt's eyes glimmered, fine lines crinkling around them good-naturedly. "Dad made me figure out how many descendants one pair of rabbits could have in three years when I acted that way the first time he took me hunting."

"And?" She expected him to tell her to figure it out herself.

"Thirteen million," he cheerfully replied. "Believe me, the farmers would have appreciated my getting rid of that one."

"But they won't know. *I* will."

Matt lifted a brow, as if challenging her assumption that he should care what she thought.

She blushed.

He offered her a hand. "I think we should be heading back. It's time to get out of the cold." He stood, pulling her with him, then stooped to pick up his bow.

The wind glued Jillian's damp jeans to her as they headed back the way they'd come. The sky seemed gray-brown, she noticed. She had no idea how long they'd been out, but it couldn't be that late. The bitter cold nipped at her face. "Is it going to snow again?" she wondered out loud.

"Probably." Matt increased his speed. "I doubt it'll be as rough as the storm last night." They didn't say anything else until they almost reached the cabin.

Jillian used the silence to think about the subject they were going to have to address soon. "If the electricity is still off tonight, it's your turn for the bedroom."

Matt stopped beside the back porch. "Are you kidding?" He pulled a shovel from beneath the steps. "Would you run in and bring out a couple of containers? We need some snow."

Jillian threw him a questioning look but did as he asked, returning with a plastic dishpan and a bright orange two-gallon bucket. "What are you doing?" she ventured, as he used the shovel to scrape the hard crust off a drift at the corner of the cabin.

"Making an ice chest out of the refrigerator." He placed the bucket on the ground and filled it with snow. "We'll set the milk directly in the dishpan and put bowls of snow around everything else."

She watched, impressed. She also saw her chance to get even for the snowball he'd thrown at her earlier. But she needed to clear up the other matter first.

She cleared her throat. "About the sleeping arrangements, how... What are we going to do?"

"I'm sleeping on the sofa bed. You can sleep anywhere you like."

Selfish lout. "The floor will be too cold."

"And hard." He leaned on the shovel handle, gazing reflectively at her. She thought she detected a smirk beneath the placid exterior of his face.

"Maybe we could take turns between the couch and chair."

"Uh-uh. You're welcome to share with me." This time he grinned, showing white teeth against his tanned skin. "I don't usually bite." He pushed the full bucket aside and began filling the green dishpan.

"I wouldn't be able to sleep."

"I didn't say we'd sleep." A low chuckle vibrated through his words. "We can consider it a test of character."

"I didn't mean that," she said and gave up. She'd tried, and his attitude banished any second thoughts she might have had about her retaliation. She waited for the perfect moment.

He moved one foot higher on the drift to balance himself as he returned to filling the dishpan with snow.

"Here, let me take that."

Jillian reached for the shovel as Matt bent to pick up the dishpan. Putting the end of the handle between his feet, she pulled gently. She didn't want to cripple him—just see him facedown in the snow.

His lower foot came sliding. With his hands full, he wavered momentarily, trying to catch his balance. She yanked the handle away in time to enjoy his slow-motion sprawl into the middle of the snowdrift. The dishpan skied down slowly, halting at her feet. Unplanned, she added the crowning touch, dumping its contents over his head. He made a perfect snow angel except for one arm. It was buried to the shoulder from his attempt to catch himself.

"That's for the snowball." She giggled, enjoying herself so much she almost forgot to run.

He recovered swiftly. One nimble move, and he was up. Her slight head start got her to the cabin as his foot hit the bottom porch step. The door slammed in his face.

He watched through the window as she swiftly turned the lock. Pleased that his look contained a challenge instead of fury—it *was* a dirty trick—she smiled. "I'll let you in if you promise no paybacks."

He shook his head.

"We're even. You got me earlier, remember?"

"One snowball." His index finger and thumb modeled a three-inch circle in the air. "One little snowball." Plucking a handful of snow from the neck of his ski suit, he held it toward her. "This isn't even."

She couldn't contain her laughter. "You look like a snowman."

"You don't have the heart to let me freeze to death."

"Wanna bet?"

One end of his mustache twitched as he lifted a gloved hand skyward. "It's snowing again."

Two flakes spit against the window as if she needed divine verification. She hadn't figured him to be a stubborn idiot on top of everything else. She nervously shifted her weight from foot to foot.

"If the door's not unlocked by the time I get back with the bucket, the compensation goes up." Matt leaped down off the porch. "Think about it." Beautifully straight teeth glimmered in a devilish smile. Then he disappeared around the corner of the house.

CHAPTER FOUR

JILLIAN STARED after him, chewing the corner of her lip. No doubt about it, Matt was insane. If he wanted to stay outside and freeze instead of agreeing to call everything even, who was she to argue? So why did she have this nagging suspicion she'd unlock the door the minute he reappeared?

"Boo!"

She almost went through the window. She hadn't expected him to materialize behind her. Clutching her chest, she sagged against the corner he'd backed her into.

He eyed her and jangled the keys in front of her nose. "I didn't even need them," he mocked. "The front door wasn't locked." He closed in on her, his eyes warm and wicked. Snow sloshed from his boots onto the linoleum floor.

She lunged toward the counter, hoping to escape past him.

He sidestepped to cut her off.

Gazing at her only other route to safety, she caught a glimpse of his sly grin. He *wanted* her to go for the door. *Go ahead,* she could almost see him think, *I'll have you swimming in snow.* Or better yet, he'd lock her out. She didn't have her keys.

Exasperated, Jillian crossed her arms over her chest and plopped down in the corner. He could pick her up and carry her outside, but she was resolved not to go quietly.

Matt hunched down beside her, accepting her silent challenge with a delighted purr. Jillian curled into a ball, wrapping her arms around her knees and hunching her shoulders.

Grabbing the collar of her heavy jacket, he tried to hitch an arm beneath her knees. He bungled the attempt and she rolled away, wedging herself between the wall and the counter.

"Dammit, Jillian, this isn't going to do you any good." She gazed up at him to smile at the frustration in his voice. There he stood, his feet planted wide apart, his hands on his slender hips, looking more handsome than ever.

She grew weak at the sight of him and squeezed her eyelids shut, concentrating on catching her breath. Slowly. Deeply. Inhale. Exhale.

He muttered to himself. She giggled nervously, hoping he was tired of the game and would go play elsewhere.

He was on his knees now, so close she sensed his slightest intake of air. She prayed her heavy coat would ward off the sensation if he touched her. She tingled just anticipating his next move.

"Give up?" she asked breathlessly.

"No," he answered, his jaw squaring. "Do you?" The gleam returned to his eyes. "Do you think you can hold that position—" he paused for effect, his mustache curved upward "—upside down?"

He proceeded to lift her from the floor by her ankles and she unfolded. Her red knit cap fell, letting her hair sweep the floor as he stood dangling her in front of him.

"Put me down." She arched her back.

His grasp tightened on her ankles. "Ya gonna go quietly, lady?" he asked from the side of his mouth.

"What do you think?" She renewed her struggle.

"I think you're more trouble than you're worth," he said quietly, lowering her gently till she was lying flat on the floor.

Sighing, she savored her victory. But only for the instant it took to look up. He towered over her, his legs straddling her hips. She didn't have time to think of moving as he swooped down, slipping one arm behind her neck, the other behind her knees. She was off the floor and in his arms in the twinkling of his eyes. Held high against his chest she felt his heart thudding. Hers began a counter beat.

Her body flowed over him. Her legs curved around his arm, her hair fanned over his shoulder. Her head felt light. She had to rest it against his chest, near his muscled neck.

She watched his throat, mesmerized, as he swallowed several times, then her eyes drifted to his mouth. His tongue moved in slow motion across his full lower lip.

She could feel longing emanating from him as surely as he must have felt its waves coming from her.

His mouth edged closer. She turned in his arms, her lips parting expectantly.

He groaned and released her legs as suddenly as he'd picked her up. Her feet slid to the ground. Every centimeter of her body came alive as it grazed his, and the arm that still held her tightened, crushing her breasts against his chest. "I can't do it," he murmured, focusing his attention on her dry lips.

She licked them and he thrust her away. "I just don't have the heart to give you the snow bath you deserve." He ran his fingers through his damp hair. "I guess Grandma's still watching over you."

Jillian breathed for the first time in what seemed like hours. *Plug me in, I can light up the whole damn cabin,* she thought dizzily. Her blood sang through her veins and her body hummed like an electric wire.

He went outside, returning with the containers of snow. Opening the refrigerator, he jammed them in.

Several minutes later, Jillian heard the shower. As soon as he finished, she'd take one herself. She didn't know what she might say, how she would act. Right now, she still wished he'd kissed her. While she listened for the water to stop, she put away the Christmas leftovers.

Was she crazy enough to risk what she had with Harrison simply because Matt played her emotions like a brass band and made her forget common sense? Harrison would never have behaved like that, struggling with her—maybe she liked the rough stuff.

That idea was ludicrous. Underlying every one of Matt's moves was a basic gentleness. He wasn't afraid to laugh, or to forget his dignity—or to touch. Jillian's heart lurched. That, combined with his captivating grin and honest eyes, made him almost irresistible.

Who wouldn't be fascinated with him? And knowing that this disorienting attraction was mutual made the situation as combustible as an unlit match in a burning matchbook.

As long as she kept her distance, she wasn't hurting anyone. But she had to remember she wasn't free to act on her dangerous fantasies.

Harrison had been a long way from her mind all day, she admitted with an uneasy twinge. She should be thinking about *his* virtues.

WHEN SHE FINISHED her shower, Jillian returned to the kitchen, curious about the muted curses she'd been hearing. She discovered Matt with his head in the oven, a pile of burnt matches beside him. "Damn," he said, bumping his head as he drew back. He eyed her sapphire-blue jumpsuit. "Nice." He frowned and looked back into the oven.

She flushed, not wanting him to think she'd dressed up for him. "I didn't exactly bring appropriate clothes for being snowed in in a cabin with a stranger," she explained nervously. "At least this shows off my new necklace." As he stood up, she glanced at the delicate bells and self-consciously touched the rounded neckline that stopped just above the gentle slope of her breasts. "I love my present. I can't tell you how much it means to me."

He didn't respond.

"You said this was a sample? You must represent a very exclusive company."

He fiddled with a small casserole sitting on the counter. "I don't represent anyone. I have contracts with several craftsmen. They supply my stores."

"Your stores?" In his worn flannel shirts and faded blue jeans—faded from wash and wear instead of bought that way—he didn't look like a businessman.

He laughed at her surprise. "Seven of them, actually. Ever heard of Carson's?"

"Carson's?" There was a Carson's Fine Jewelry in Topeka. It was one of a chain.

He answered with a nod and put whatever he'd been making into the oven. He pulled it back out as soon as he'd pushed it in. "I can't light this damned oven!"

He didn't take defeat gracefully, she noted.

"I've thought I had it lit twice now, but it's out again."

Pleased that she could finally do something for him, she reached for a match. He caught her hand before she could strike it. "I've had the gas on. Don't you think we'd better wait?"

She hadn't thought clearly since he'd entered the cabin late last night, but wasn't about to admit that to him. "It wasn't on very long." She leaned against the counter. "Let me know when you think it's safe."

His wry smile hinted that he knew he was making her crazy.

"How about a glass of wine while we wait? What do you think? Rosé or white?"

"I don't know what we're having for dinner."

"It's a cranberry and turkey casserole my dad always made with the leftovers."

She wrinkled her nose. "Sounds awful."

"That's what everyone thinks until they try it. You'll love it."

"I guess you'd better make it white. I don't know what goes with cranberries."

Her answer irritated him for some reason. "Why don't you choose what you prefer instead of what's proper?"

"I don't have a preference. Grandma was pretty straitlaced about drinking and so I'm not much of a wine connoisseur. I have to rely on trying to pick whatever is appropriate." She refused to be baited by what sounded like an accusation.

"You don't *have* to have either," he said, but reached into the cabinet and brought out a couple of jelly glasses, holding them out for her inspection. "Fine crystal for milady?" he mocked, taking down one of the wine bottles from the cabinet over the refrigerator.

"Is there something wrong with wanting to do the right thing?" she asked, annoyed.

"Only if you're doing it for that reason alone."

Jillian tilted her head defiantly. "I grew up in a small town where even the cream of the crop weren't exactly 'high society.' Grandma taught me not to eat peas with a knife and all that, but I've had to work hard at learning 'the right thing.'"

"That's important to you?" Matt's tone softened considerably, but still held an edge.

She nodded. "Sometimes. I like feeling I can handle myself in any situation."

"Knowing the 'right thing' insures that?"

His skeptical look reminded her of the way she'd "handled" this whole mess and her mortification at her earlier behavior grew. She shrugged helplessly and decided to disregard his touchy mood. "Do you realize you change the subject when we start to talk about you?'' she asked as he opened the white wine and poured them each a measure.

"I didn't know we were talking about me."

"We were talking about your stores."

"That's about as mundane a topic as you'll find."

"How did you get into that business?" She felt the tension between them ease. "I never would have pictured you as a jeweler."

He swished his wine around in the glass before answering. "It's a long story," he warned.

She waved at the window. The snow was dropping in giant flakes. "I'm not going anywhere." Leaning down to cup her chin in her hand, she propped her elbow on the counter and added, "I may have even talked to you before. Carson's is where my boss buys all his wife's gifts. And he orders your specialty items when he needs a present for a visiting bigwig."

"The senator has an account with us," he nodded.

Waiting for him to continue was an exercise in futility. She wanted to strangle him. "So?" She sighed, exasperated. "How did you get into the jewelry business?"

He squinted as if trying to remember. "I spent a lot of time at one of the neighbor's after my mom left. Dad spent every free moment at the local pool hall, so I kind of adopted the man next door for company. He'd been silversmithing for years, as a hobby. We lived in Colorado, near several abandoned mines, and he'd go find his own silver, refine it—everything— then sit for hours shaping it into some beautiful piece of jewelry." Matt glanced at his watch. "It's time to light the oven."

"Uh-uh," she objected, shaking her head. "You aren't going to change the subject again that easily. You talk, I'll light."

He glanced at her sardonically, but continued. "John's specialty was delicate butterfly earrings. No two pairs alike, but you couldn't tell one from the other in a set. They always matched perfectly. It fascinated me."

Jillian smiled. He was in some distant past now, and his eyes were seeing something she couldn't. She quietly slid the casserole into the oven and lifted herself onto the counter across from him.

"You have to understand, John was in his early seventies at the time, but still a burly, big man with a voice like thunder. Most of the kids in town shied away from his end of the block. He was the bad example mothers used if their kids didn't toe the line. You know—the town 'bogeyman.' He had several old cars in his backyard. No semblance of a lawn—even in summer—just waist-high weeds everywhere except the path to his door."

She pictured Matt, a lonely little boy, deserted by his mother—and technically by his father, too, from the sound of things—turning to a gruff old man for companionship.

"How high did you set the oven?" Matt brought her thoughts back to practicalities.

"Three-fifty?"

He nodded. "I'll set the timer. We may as well sit in the other room."

Jillian waited for Matt to finish and then followed him into the other room, sitting opposite him at the end of the couch. Drawing her feet under her, she leaned forward. "I take it *you* didn't think John was the bogeyman."

He laughed. "Remind me to fix you one of his famous Tom and Jerrys later. Would the bogeyman let me, and two or three of the bravest boys, have our Tom and Jerrys laced with rum once a year at Christmas time? We felt we were in on some very grown-up rite."

Jillian realized that he didn't share these memories often, or with just anyone. "I'll bet if your parents knew, they would have lynched him."

"And I'll bet he didn't put in as much as a teaspoon. But it was the thought that counted with us. We were big-time." He smiled wistfully.

He was "grown-up" at nine or ten, she guessed, while she'd practically been a baby at eighteen when she left for secretarial college. No wonder he'd ridiculed her inability to choose a wine. He'd probably been making most of his own decisions since his mother took off. The thought made her sad.

"So explain about John and the jewelry," she urged.

"John had an amazing amount of patience with me. He always asked if I had my homework done before I could stay and watch him work. At first, I thought he was trying to get rid of me. It took me a while to figure out that he wasn't." He ran his finger idly around the edge of his glass. "He insisted on seeing my report card at the end of every term. Then, if I'd done well, I got to 'help' him make something. Usually a ring with a stone setting since that was the easiest. As I got better, he'd let me do my own. It took him longer to face the fact that I'd never be an artist than it did me."

His voice changed and he was back with her again. He gave her a sheepish grin, "Oh, I loved what he created, so I tried, but I got more pleasure from digging around in his vast stock and sorting it out. I even made little wooden cases in Dad's workshop for all of it. When I'd ask what he was going to do with his forty-odd years' collection, he'd growl and say, 'It's a hobby, boy. I guess I'll let someone else worry about throwing them away when I'm gone.'"

Matt's gravelly rendition gave her an image of the man.

"I was about fifteen when I asked if I could sell some of it for him. He and his wife had only been married a couple of years when she died. With his biggest admirer in her grave, he'd just make things and set them aside. He didn't think I'd have any luck, but agreed to let me try, and I began—"

The timer went off, and Matt looked startled, then relieved. He led the way back to the kitchen and asked her to set the table. "I'll finish getting this ready," he said, finding the blue-checked mitt and opening the oven door. Within five minutes, they were seated.

"It *looks* all right," Jillian said skeptically.

"It smells so good." Matt breathed the fruity aroma deeply.

Jillian took a bite. "It's nice," she agreed, pleasantly surprised, but anxious to get back on the subject. "So you started selling John's pieces?"

"That's about it."

"No," she protested. "You were just beginning to explain how that turned into a business. John sounds..." Like the answer to a lonely young boy's prayers, she said silently. "Wonderful," she finished aloud.

Matt laughed. "He'd roll over in his grave. He thought he kept his reputation intact right up until he died six years ago." His sigh was a mixture of fond memories and melancholy. "He probably did, except with a few of us."

Jillian wanted to cover his hand with hers. She wished she could comfort him as he had comforted her earlier this afternoon. But she wasn't sure he'd appreciate it. "You cared a great deal for him," she whispered.

"I did."

"How did selling his jewelry go?" she asked after a moment.

"Have you ever considered becoming a newspaper reporter?" he teased. "You'd be great at digging up everyone's dirt."

She rubbed her hands together. "There's dirt coming?"

"Yeah." He leaned forward, lowering his voice conspiratorially. "The local jeweler asked me nicely to quit and I figured I must be cutting into his business."

"You weren't," she replied with mock horror.

"I was," he admitted, eyes twinkling. "So I offered him first chance at everything I sold."

He spoke so quietly that Jillian had to inch closer to catch his words.

"John must have had a lot to sell after forty years. Let me guess," Jillian whispered in return. "You double-crossed John, kept all the money and started buying stores."

"He split the profits with me." Matt pushed back in his chair as if the game had suddenly grown old. "We were partners."

Jillian started to interrupt with a question and he rushed on as if in a hurry to finish. "I saved my share and bought parts for one of his old cars and began fixing that up.

"Since I couldn't sell to anyone locally except old Mr. Hatfield, once I had the car running, I drove to other towns and sold to jewelers there. Of course, I'd raised the prices by then. Mr. Hatfield charged his customers the earth, or so I thought at the time, but John's designs sold out regularly."

Matt tipped his chair back on two legs and spread his hands in a "that's that" gesture.

Jillian shook her head exasperatedly. "That still doesn't tell me how you ended up with seven jewelry stores."

He grinned at her thoughtfully. "I guess it doesn't, does it?"

"No."

He looked like a clam slowly closing up.

"I'll take the short version if you insist," she said hastily, but couldn't resist adding, "It's not like we've got anything better to do."

He looked as though he wanted to disagree, then shrugged. "I started representing several more craftsmen. Then I expanded to selling in four states. I used the money to pay my way through college, got a degree in retail management, and watched for an opportunity to buy a store. The first one was in Emporia.

I gradually bought other stores." He stood up from the table. "The last two were planned expansions. I built the ones in Wichita and Colorado Springs." He stopped talking abruptly.

"Where do you live?" She sensed his growing impatience but was reluctant to let him break off without revealing any present history. "How do you manage so many stores when they're all scattered around like that?"

"Sometimes it gets a little complicated." He answered the last question noncommittally, and ignored the first. "Shall we clean up this mess?"

She began stacking dishes. "How did your father react to your little business? What happened to it after he died?"

He held up a hand when she would have continued. "What is this? Twenty questions? Didn't anyone ever tell you what happened to the cat? If you ever need a career other than little miss homemaker or the politician's socially correct little assistant, you could become a private detective or newspaper reporter extraordinaire." He took the dishrag out of her hand and gave her the towel. "Your turn to dry," he instructed, running the water. "I always hated that job. I think parents give it to kids because they hate it, too."

That's all you're going to get, Jillian, his expression said. *For now,* she almost added aloud. When the dishes were finished and put away, Matt folded the towel.

"It's early yet." She looked at her watch. The dim lantern light made it seem later. "Much too early for bed," she tacked on.

"Depends on what you're going to do there." Suddenly, all the earlier tension was back.

Her color deepened. "What would you like to do?"

"Bad question," he answered, his eyes steady on her lips.

"I mean right now."

"It's still a bad question." He grinned and lowered his eyes to take in her gentle curves as she looked nervously away.

"You must have planned something for this week. What were you going to do here all by yourself?"

"Hunt, watch a little TV, read, catch up on some paperwork. With the year end right around the corner, I have plenty of that, and I've got some fair-sized decisions to make." His bold eyes rested on her neckline and a sultry heat seemed to envelop her.

She moved away, then realized he was intentionally making her self-conscious to distract her from further interrogation.

"What did you and Harrison have planned?" he asked innocently. Her face turned Santa-suit red. "Besides that."

"I brought a couple of games." She gladly changed the subject. "Would you like to play Scrabble with me?"

"I guess we could."

"Unless you'd rather read or something," she added quickly. "I brought a couple of books with me." *But I can't read them,* she admitted to herself. The books had been picked specifically to stimulate a romantic mood. And she definitely didn't need stimulating.

"Or something," he muttered under his breath. "You get it set up and ready. I'll bring in a little more wood for the night."

"My turn first?" he asked, moments later, before even taking off his coat. He stood behind his chair, looking down at the tiles on his letter rack, pulling off his gloves.

"I guess so," she agreed, looking at the conglomeration of O-R-L-D-P-V-G on her rack. If he already had a word, he was more than welcome to start. Maybe she'd have something to build on.

He put down his letters, unbuttoned and shed his coat, turning to hang it on one of the hooks by the door.

S-E-X, his word said in blinking letters, until Jillian realized it was her eyelids doing the blinking. Her eyes flew to his face as he sat down. He shrugged. "You have to use letters like X as quickly as you can or you're stuck with them at the end of the game. Besides, I can spell it. Spelling isn't one of my strong suits."

She added L-O-V to his E.

He laughed. "Oh, yes, we can't have one without the other, can we?"

She caught herself smiling, but said warily, "I'm not sure we should play this."

He shook his head. "You just want to back out because I'm winning."

"After one word?"

"Ten to seven. Who's keeping score, anyway? Shall I get you a pencil and a piece of paper?"

Jillian good-naturedly accepted his teasing, accusing him from time to time of making up or misspelling his words. "Did you bring a dictionary?" he asked when she contested the final score, taking off sixteen points for a word she was sure was wrong. "I *know* that isn't a word," she insisted, removing ARG from the board. The R had changed her word, SPA, to SPAR and the G was on a triple word space.

"Unless you can prove it's not, put it back." His hazel eyes glinted, inviting her to defy him. He fingered the corner of his mustache. "You're just a poor loser, Jake."

"Can you prove it *is* a word? What does it mean?" Her voice sounded airy. She couldn't refrain from watching his mouth and it made her breathless.

"An arg is a type of metal fastener used in putting together mechanical components," he said smoothly.

"Okay," she granted reluctantly, tearing her eyes from his face and re-adding his score. "You win. Would you like to play again?"

Shaking his head, he went into the bedroom and came back with a book. "I think I'll read."

"I guess I'll find my book," she finally said, more to herself than to him. He didn't act as though he'd heard, anyway.

The words in her book didn't make any sense, and Jillian turned pages mindlessly. The figure sitting in the chair by the flickering fire held her concentration. The glow spread an aura around him that made him seem magical, mystical. She sat across the room from him, watching him read, watching his motionless body. His book hid his face now. It seemed like a wall.

She gently laid down her novel, brooding over the space between them.

"Wouldn't you like to play another game?" she asked hopefully.

"No. I'd like to read. I didn't come here to entertain you, Jillian," he added quickly. His soft tone did nothing to soothe the tension growing inside her.

"How about something different? I've got other games besides Scrabble."

In one smooth move, he'd laid down his book and was standing beside her. His hand stroked her face. "The only thing I'd like to do with you right now is make love." His eyes bored deep into hers, as if he were seeking her soul. His voice became husky. "Is that how you'd like me to entertain you? I assure you, it would be very pleasant."

She swallowed.

His lips started a slow descent toward hers. And heaven help her, she wanted him to kiss her, to hold her, to stop this indefinable aching. Yet she pulled away, easing her face from his grip.

"I take it that's a 'no,'" he said blandly, then turned to pick up his book. "If I were you, I wouldn't push it, Jillian. You may not want the kind of attention you get from me if I concentrate on you."

Hardly conscious of what she was doing, she followed him across the room and knelt beside his chair. She ignored the warning bell sounding in the dim recesses of her mind because, suddenly, there was nothing in the world more important than having his undivided attention. Nothing. "Okay, Matt," she agreed breathlessly.

His eyes left the book and studied her intently. "No strings attached?" He echoed the phrase she'd used—was it only this morning—before accepting his gift.

"What do you mean?" she stammered.

"I mean," he spoke slowly, "if we make love, it will change nothing."

"Of course, it would change things," Jillian protested.

"Oh, yes, it would change the nature of our stay here. And it will change what happens when the boyfriend arrives. But when it's time to go back to the real world, this week will be just a very pleasant memory for me. Will you feel the same way?"

What is he asking? Her brows knitted tightly. "I'm not sure I understand." She couldn't take her eyes from his lips. It was so hard to think with her heart pounding crazily in her ears.

"If Harrison gets here, will you be able to pretend nothing happened between us?" He paused, waiting for her to answer. When she didn't, he carried on relentlessly. "If he breaks your engagement, won't you expect me to be a gentleman and step in for him?"

He reached out to smooth the lines between her brows with a fingertip. "I told you, I'm not the marrying kind. I'd hate to see you mess up whatever you have with Harrison for a roll with me, because that's all it would be. Much as I like you, Jake, I don't intend to fall into the kind of trap you are unknowingly—and I do think it's unknowingly—setting. Lord, what a trap." He swept a hand through his hair and sighed. "Shall I put the book down?"

If he makes love to me, nothing will ever be the same, Jillian admitted to herself. "I . . . You . . ." She gulped, taking on a hot flush that threatened to burn her to a cinder. "I know you're right," she said finally, standing up and backing away, "but I wish . . . I wish you weren't."

CHAPTER FIVE

"I'M NUTS," Jillian muttered as she stumbled through the bedroom and into the bathroom. Her cheeks burned, despite the room's icy temperature, and she laid the back of her hand across her forehead to see if she had a temperature.

She did. She definitely had a temperature. But she knew that it wasn't caused by anything other than the man in the room out there and her own mortifying behavior. Whatever had possessed her?

She shivered and began peeling off the velvety blue jumpsuit. Its soft texture intensified the screaming of her nerve endings as it slid to the floor. She jerked on the sweat suit she'd decided to sleep in, hoping the coarser fabric and even rougher treatment would put an end to the tingling of her sensitized skin. How could she have behaved so shamelessly?

Jillian's eyes were drawn to the pale but flushed face in the mirror. In the dim candlelight, the blue eyes looked confused and luminescent. The heart-shaped mouth trembled. Her blond mop of hair fluffed out around her face in wild disarray. She looked like one of those women in perfume commercials who were preparing for a big seduction scene. *Lord, what he must think of me!* She turned away from her reflection.

She didn't think much of herself, either. What did she think she was doing? Why, a couple of days ago she was worrying about being frigid! Now, twenty-four hours with a heartbreaker and she was throwing herself practically at his feet, begging him to make love to her. *He probably imagines I've been carrying on with all and sundry all my life!*

And she'd totally forgotten about Harrison. She gulped back a sob and closed her eyes, refusing to give in to tears. She could face making a fool of herself, but she wasn't sure she'd be able to face Harrison. Time and again, she'd avoided Harrison's advances, yet just now, she'd made one of her own—to someone else.

"Jillian?"

She jumped at the sound of Matt's voice, trying to pull herself together and respond naturally. Her own voice wouldn't come.

"Are you all right?"

"Fine. Just fine," she answered much too brightly.

She heard him press against the closed door and instinctively leaned away, as if she'd felt his weight.

"You're sure?" He sounded concerned.

"I'm just finishing my nightly rituals." There. That was the right touch of casual nonchalance. She hoped it allayed his worry.

"Okay," he said finally. She heard hesitant-sounding footsteps recede.

Well, she'd better start preparing for sleep, she supposed—she couldn't hide in the bathroom forever.

Sleep? How could she sleep? If an uneasy conscience didn't keep her awake, worry would. What was wrong with her? She gave her fine flyaway hair an extra hundred strokes. Her teeth wouldn't stop chattering. She clenched them. The chill finally forced her to return to the warmth of the living room.

The armload of bedding she clutched couldn't shield her from Matt's steady gaze. She heard him put down his book, and get to his feet, so she wasn't surprised when he peeled away the layers of blankets masking her face. He studied her, assessing the damage, she assumed, but she was careful to avoid his eyes. Wordlessly, they pulled out and made the bed.

As she crawled under the covers, Matt resettled in the chair and picked up his book.

He'd taken off his sweater and rolled up his shirtsleeves past his elbows. The golden hair on his strong forearms shimmered in the firelight.

"Go to sleep, Jillian." She jumped at his voice, which carried a hint of warning. She closed her eyes and tried. Anything less than total unconsciousness just wouldn't do.

Much later an unfamiliar heaviness woke her. Matt was not only beside her in the bed, he had somehow surrounded her. She tingled, tensed and then allowed herself to relax against his chest. She mentally mapped their positions.

He'd fitted himself against her like a piece of an interlocking puzzle. Her neck rested on his arm and his hand curled around hers. His knees were bent into hers.

Experimentally, she shifted her top knee. His leg followed as if magnetized. His other arm encircled her shoulders and his hand dangled lightly against her breasts.

She ought to move, but his warm steady breathing fanned her neck comfortably. Besides, what would happen if she woke him? She couldn't count on his self-restraint forever, and she couldn't trust herself to be levelheaded either—last evening certainly proved that.

Since yesterday, she'd been suppressing wild imaginings of him as her tutor in the art of love. She didn't dare give those ideas the chance of becoming reality.

His hand left her breast, smoothing her hair away from his face. She held her breath. His head nudged nearer until she felt his mouth millimeters from her ear. It was torture. But a special kind of torture, she admitted to herself.

He seemed very comfortable. How many women had he slept with this way? Judging from what Karen had said, probably more than his share. His arm returned to its earlier resting place, but this time, his hand curved around her breast. *Enough is enough!* she thought desperately, trying to ignore her body's response. Now she *had* to move.

She tried to slip away. His hand glided down to tighten around her waist. His forearm flexed, drawing her closer. Was he awake? She shivered, praying that he wasn't. The even rise and fall of his chest resumed and she relaxed. Now she could feel every line of his heart-stoppingly hard body against her back, but she didn't dare try to move again. The consequences could be disastrous.

Jillian forced herself to take slow even breaths. As she relaxed, she instinctively pressed closer to Matt, enjoying his protection and warmth. This *could* be nice, she thought.

Her mouth curved into a wisp of a contented smile as she closed her eyes and willed herself back to sleep.

THE NEXT MORNING Matt was gone. After an initial attack of panic, Jillian felt relieved at not having to face him. His Blazer still leaned drunkenly out of the same snowdrift it had been in since Christmas Eve, so she knew he hadn't gone far. Finding a note stating that he'd be back for lunch, calmed any lingering fears. She wandered around aimlessly for a bit, then did a few chores, finally settling in for a day's work on Grandma's quilt.

When he came in for lunch he had red ears, what looked like a frostbitten nose and a surly disposition. She didn't ask where he'd been. Instead, she ladled out the chili she'd prepared. Whenever she opened her mouth to say something, he growled at her, so she kept her peace. She passed him her homemade rolls and they ate in silence.

Then, he returned to the bedroom and came back with his still-damp outdoor gear. "Where are you going?" she asked and immediately wished she hadn't.

"Back out," he replied, heading for the door.

"What did you do all morning?"

He pulled his boots over his thick socks, ignoring her.

Darn it, while he *was* here, she was going to make sure she heard a human voice, even if it was only hers. She lowered her voice an octave. "I had a lovely morning, Jillian, tromping about in the snow. Would you like to come with me?"

Matt gave her a look that could have scorched a chestnut. "Now Mama and Papa Bear will go for a walk. Right?"

She frowned and backed away at his bitter tone. "What did I do?" She'd worked so hard at keeping everything friendly yet impersonal.

"What didn't you do? You mopped floors and made a hot lunch. For good measure, you threw in homemade rolls, smiled pleasantly across the table and pretended not to be bothered by my mood." He continued sarcastically. "Would you like a printed agenda of my day? Shouldn't Mama Bear know what Papa Bear is up to? That would complete the perfect picture, wouldn't it?"

Her jaw dropped.

"I'm not interested in playing house with you, Jillian, however attractive you make the picture seem." He bit out his words emphatically. "This is all good bait—but not for me. I can do all *that* for myself. Now if you really want to do something for me..." he taunted, coming toward her menacingly.

"Of all the conceited, arrogant—" She couldn't think of any names insulting enough to call him. "That wasn't bait! I did all that because it needed to be done. The rolls were made and frozen weeks ago— long before I knew you. What an egomaniac!"

He eyed her suspiciously, then threw up his hands. "Ignore me, Jake." His voice softened for the first time since he'd returned. "I'm in a bad mood."

"I noticed." Jillian wanted to approach him, but kept her feet firmly planted in the center of the room. "Why?"

"Chalk it up to exhaustion. I didn't sleep well."

"You seemed to."

His brow shot up and she flushed.

"I didn't think you knew I came to bed."

"I woke up once. You were sleeping like a baby." Jillian couldn't meet his eyes. Her body warmed at the memory of the way he'd held her while he slept.

"Maybe for a while, but you kept me awake most of the night. Every time I'd get to sleep, I'd wake to find you plastered against me. Heaven help poor Harry. He's going to spend the rest of his life walking around like the living dead."

Jillian didn't argue, although *he* had kept her "plastered" to him. She decided that wasn't a safe subject. "Can I go back outside with you?"

"It's much too cold."

"You don't seem to mind," she pressed.

"I'm used to it."

"I won't bother you," she promised.

"You'd bother me," he assured her, shaking his head as he yanked on a ski cap.

"Will you at least tell me what you've been doing?" He raised an eyebrow, questioning her right to ask. "Pure and simple curiosity. I'm not checking up on you. But I'm going to go stark raving mad if someone doesn't talk to me."

"I'm looking for a way out of here," he said. "I walked out to the county road. It looks like they've cleared those. This afternoon I'm going to try to find someone with a functioning phone on the other side of the lake. All the homes this side of the point are closed for the winter." He shrugged and zipped his coat. "Maybe I'll be luckier this afternoon." He paused in the act of opening the door. "You'll be all right?"

"Sure." She turned her back to him.

"Sure," he echoed. "That's why you're pouting."

She lifted a shoulder and stretched her hands toward the fireplace. "I'm not. It's just so quiet out here. I feel like I must be the only one left in the world."

His hand on her arm surprised her. She hadn't heard him cross the room. "You're not alone, Jake."

"I know," she said, resisting the urge to fling herself at him and beg him to stay. "I'm beginning to go a little nuts."

"Me, too," he muttered under his breath, and dropped his arm. "I'll be back before dark."

Jillian straightened everything up again and resumed her quilting. She'd brought the quilt with her, hoping to finally get some work done on it. Whenever she'd attempted to work on it before, she'd dissolved into tears, memories rushing in on her as she touched the fabric. She had cut pieces from some of her grandmother's dresses, which one of her elderly neighbors in Topeka had sewn into a patterned quilt top. Jillian planned to make the kind of quilt Grandma had made from Jillian's baby clothes. It would be a keepsake for her daughter. A memory of the great-grandmother she'd never meet. This first Christmas with Harrison had seemed an appropriate time to work on the quilt.

After a few false starts and a few wistful sighs about the quality of her stitches compared with Grandma's, memories—happy ones this time—engrossed her, and the afternoon flew.

This square of floral print was from one of the dresses Grandma wore when she went "out." This one, Grandma had worn the night Jillian graduated.

She smiled, remembering Grandma's exuberance that—

Jillian jumped as Matt poked his head around the kitchen door. "I didn't realize the woodpile was depleted. I'm going to have to cut some more." He stuck a snowy boot into the room. "Will you get me the chain saw out of the utility closet? I don't want to track up your clean floor." He scowled at the few lonely logs next to the fireplace. "It's going to be cold tonight."

"Do you want some help?"

"No need, I'll just bring back enough to see us through the night. We'll build up the supply tomorrow if we can't manage to find a way out by then." The sky darkened as he spoke. "I'd better get going if I don't want to be lugging wood back after dark."

"I'll start supper," Jillian offered, handing him the saw.

"It's my turn, but I'll trade you for tomorrow."

He seemed to be in a better mood now and she mirrored his smile. The sun and wind had burned his face, making it shine in the fading light. She hadn't noticed the tiny laugh lines around his eyes until the sun had highlighted them, reddening everything but narrow white streaks. She reached automatically to touch them, excusing herself to both of them by remarking on the sunburn. She gave herself permission to let her hand linger. "Does it hurt?"

His expression darkened and she drew her hand away. "It'll be tan by tonight," he murmured.

Opening the door, he paused—half in, half out—as if reluctant to leave. "Things going better this afternoon?" he asked.

She nodded and indicated the quilt frame in the main room. It suddenly occurred to her that this was the first time she'd taken it out without crying. "I'm working on a memory quilt." She paused to clear her throat. "It's design uses some of my grandmother's things. This is the first time I've been able to get much done on it."

"That's good, Jake," he said softly. "Everything fades in time," he added, almost to himself.

Jillian closed the door behind him, watching through the window until he disappeared into the trees.

Nightfall was well on its way by the time she had supper started and turned her attention back to the quilt. She had to light the lantern to see her delicate stitches.

As she worked her mind turned to the future but Harrison, the man who should have filled her thoughts, had somehow become a shadowy figure.

She listened absentmindedly to the distant clatter of the chain saw and let Matt take the spotlight in her thoughts.

Anyone could go a little overboard for Prince Charming, especially at close quarters. And Matt was a fairy-tale hero who had saved her from a lonely Christmas. Their isolation made the real world seem like a dream. Once they left, she wouldn't even remember this intense feeling of belonging to him. No one could live a lifetime in fantasy land, she reminded herself.

Jillian winced. She'd stabbed herself with the needle. "I'm going to have to pay attention to what I'm doing or quit," she muttered, watching the blood bead on her fingertip. An uneasiness washed over her and she frowned. She raised her head, and a drop of blood fell on the quilt, unheeded. What was different?

The chain saw sputtered, echoing her discordant thoughts. It groaned unevenly.

Something was wrong. Something had happened. It was dark and Matt should have been back by now. The chain saw had changed its tune from a hypnotic buzz to an intermittent whine. The hair stood up on the back of her neck.

She grabbed the flashlight from the shelf in the utility closet and jerked on her ski jacket and boots. Night had replaced day. The temperature was probably dropping by the minute. If something *had* happened, it would take very little time for Matt to freeze to death.

She plunged out into the night, calling Matt's name. The wind whipped the sound away, leaving her engulfed in bitter cold and a strange silence—made stranger by the monotonous whine of the saw. Playing the beam from the flashlight around her, she followed his footprints down a snowy path.

Minutes later, she lurched to an uneasy stop. He'd probably made several sets of tracks in the snow during the day. What if she couldn't find him? She clamped down on her rising horror. Panic wouldn't do either of them any good. *Listen,* she ordered herself, and the churning mechanical note of the saw led her down an embankment and toward the lake.

The ground was rougher here. Snakelike tree roots packed with a mixture of snow and ice made each step seem like an act of defiance, and the icy wind stiffened her muscles.

She heard the chain saw more clearly now, and homed in on the sound. Its motor droned in time to her footsteps. Slipping on an especially icy patch, she grabbed an overhanging branch and the flashlight cast random patterns around her. The beam of light passed over—then jerked back to—a figure about ten yards away.

Matt was lying facedown on the ground, surrounded by scattered logs. The yellow chain saw lay a short distance from his head. She gasped and tried to run. Slipping, she reverted to tormentingly slow motion to keep from falling.

The saw blinked like a caution signal as it reflected the shaking flashlight's beam. She held her breath, her heart thudding heavily as she at last reached his still figure. Staring in horror at the widening dark spot in the white snow, she made a lunge for the diabolical-looking saw and switched it off. Her trembling legs wouldn't hold her as its moaning finally settled into silence.

She fell to her knees beside him, hesitating, afraid to touch him, frightened of what she might find. Then he groaned, and she sagged across his back in relief. "Matt," she whispered, swiping at a tear and grasping his shoulders. She tried to turn him. "Matt?" By nudging her knees under his side, she managed to get the necessary leverage to ease him onto his back.

The unexpectedly small gash above one of his eyebrows ran a river of dark blood into his hair, then dripped onto the snow. "Oh, Matt! Oh, Matt!" she chanted, rubbing his face with a handful of snow. She felt angry and helpless until he groaned again, spit out an oath and opened his eyes. "Thank heaven. I thought you were going to die on me."

He smiled weakly and her heart faltered. "Wishful thinking?" he asked hoarsely.

She half smiled. "Lord, you scared me." She pushed the words past the lump clogging her voice.

"I slipped." He winced as she pitched the saw farther away to give them more room. "If you want to get vicious, take it out on that tree."

She gingerly touched the skin above the wound and satisfied herself that his injury wasn't as bad as all the blood suggested. "You may have a concussion." She spoke more to herself than to him as he waved her away and tried to sit up. She frowned. Should she move him? "You'd better stay still."

"We're going to freeze to death if I stay still." He raised himself on his elbow and she nodded in agreement. She braced him while he turned on his side. He drew his knees under him, then wavered.

"You're dizzy," she accused.

"A little." He gave her a tight grin and resumed his effort to stand.

Draping one of his arms over her shoulder, she tried to take his weight. "Don't you dare pass out on me, Matt Carson."

"I'll be fine," he promised quietly. "Give me a minute."

She propped him against a tree. "Let me do something about that blood." She ducked out from beneath his arm, scooping up a handful of snow to clean the cut. The bleeding seemed to have lessened a little, she thought hopefully.

"Ready to try again?" she asked, repositioning herself at his side. He nodded. "Lean on me. We'll go slowly."

With one arm around his waist, she half led, half dragged him, holding the flashlight with her free hand. They picked their way through the brittle undergrowth and back to the steep path. "Wait a minute." He stopped her and picked up a handful of snow. "I can't see where we're going." Matt held the snow to his cut as she concentrated on finding the best footholds for them. By the time the lights from the cabin were in view through the clearing, she felt as if she'd been to the end of the earth and back. She'd never been so happy to arrive anywhere in her life.

After helping him take off his coat, she led him to a chair. The jagged wound gaped but the bleeding had stopped. "I'll look in the medicine cabinet in the bathroom. Karen surely keeps a first-aid kit here."

Returning, she almost dropped the pan of warm water and the bandages she carried. Matt had his coat back on and was squatting by the fireplace, rearranging the logs with the poker. "What do you think you're doing?"

"I've got to go back after the wood. And we left Jim's chain saw lying in the snow," he explained just as if there were nothing unusual about walking around with a hole in your head.

"Oh, no, you don't! Get back in that chair." His ready obedience was a sure indication that he didn't feel as fit as he'd like her to believe. She sank to her knees beside him. "What am I going to do if you pass out on me again, Matt? Have you thought about that?'' She chewed worriedly at the edge of her lip. ''I can't lift you. I can't call an ambulance.''

''I'll manage,'' he assured her.

''How will you manage if you're out cold? It will be *my* problem.'' She wiggled her thumb to show him the roll of adhesive tape she'd dropped over it and set the pan of water on the hearth. ''You're about to see the extent of my first aid, and you're worried about a chain saw?''

''Are you trying to tell me I'm not in good hands?'' he teased, then added grimly, ''I'm more worried about the wood.''

She ignored his comment, pushed his head back against the chair and wrung out the washcloth she'd brought. In her irritation, she forgot to be gentle as she cleansed his wound. ''Sorry,'' she muttered at his ''ouch'' and eased up.

He laughed quietly. ''Sure you are. I'd hate to have you mad at me, Jake.''

His good humor made her feel a little brighter. It would obviously take more than an accident to get him down. ''I *am* mad at you. You could have picked a better time and place to try to kill yourself. I think I should try to drive my car out. You need to see a doctor.''

He shook his head vigorously, wincing at the pain it caused.

''I might be able to get to the roads they've cleared. It's worth trying. I'm afraid of what might happen to you if you have a concussion.''

''I don't have a concussion,'' he denied, as she finished scrubbing the wound.

"You're certain of that, Dr. Carson?" She held the bandage in place, taped it, then took it off and started over. "You need stitches," she muttered disgustedly. "You'll have to help me. Keep the edges of the cut together while I put on the bandage." He pinched the raw edges in place and she reapplied a new sterile pad and strips of adhesive.

"There." She stood up, satisfied at last. He still looked pale. "Don't you move," she commanded, picking up her supplies.

She brought sheets and blankets back with her this time, set them aside, shifted her quilt rack and unfolded the couch. A warning look held him in his chair when he would have risen to help her.

"Now, into this bed," she told him in the same kind of voice her grandmother would have used to forestall any argument.

She followed close behind as he walked around the end of the couch. If he fainted, at least she could direct his fall, she thought helplessly.

He didn't feel as well as he pretended, because he sat down to remove his coat. The blood spatters decorating it made her shiver as she pushed it aside and helped him with his boots. Then, hesitating briefly, she gripped the zipper of his ski bibs and pulled it down. Keeping her eyes fixed on his sweater, she hauled them off of him, resuming normal breathing only after she turned her back.

"You're not quitting now?" he taunted, sounding almost like his usual self. "I'm going to need help with the rest of my clothes."

"Tough." Tears of relief itched the back of her eyes and she went to the kitchen to sponge off their stained coats. He was swinging his long john-clad body under the sheet when she returned.

"Do you feel queasy at all?" she asked, exhaling slowly. She'd spent the time in the kitchen trying to remember the rules for giving first aid to head injury victims. "Would you like some turkey broth?" she offered after his negative response to the first question.

He lifted the corner of his lip in distaste.

"You shouldn't have anything to eat. You can have liquids." She raised a shoulder defensively.

"I'm glad you didn't take up nursing," he said, obviously amused by her attempts at taking care of him. "You'd probably worry your patients to death."

"I'm the first to admit I'm no Florence Nightingale. That's why I think I should try to go for help. We don't have any idea how badly you're hurt. What if something happens, Matt?"

"It won't. I'm only letting you hover over me like a mother hen to keep you from doing something drastic. I'll go along with it for a while to let you get the nurse bit out of your system. Then I've got to go back out and bring in some of that wood. That's it." He nodded toward the three lonely logs stacked in the corner. "That will never get us through the night."

"Then I'll go," Jillian said and started for the bedroom to get her coat. She remembered that it was hanging over a kitchen chair, still damp, as Matt caught her wrist.

"Uh-uh."

"But—"

"If you go, I go with you. You try to leave this cabin by yourself, Jillian, and you're going to find out I'm in a whole lot better shape than you imagine."

She lowered herself to the bed and his grip on her arm loosened. He let his fingers slide down and lightly encompass her hand.

"With the windchill, it's probably minus twenty degrees. I've been every direction today and we can't get out without walking almost five miles. In this weather that kind of trip would be suicide, and no one could get back without help from a snowplow. We'll manage."

"We'll manage better if you let me go out and pick up the logs you dropped when you fell."

"I don't fall."

She looked at him blankly. His statement didn't make sense. "The tree attacked you, I suppose?" She suddenly remembered one of the things you had to watch for with a head injury. Lord, was he losing touch with reality?

He looked at the dismay on her face and grinned. "I guess I should say that if I couldn't make it back without an accident, neither could you. And don't accuse me of male chauvinism. But I can't remember any other time when I've slipped and fallen on ice." He held up a finger to stop her interruption, covering her lips gently. "I have great balance. And I know that path. Jim and I went up and down it at least ten times a day last summer when we were here fishing."

She remembered his catlike grace and understood. "But *I'm* not exactly uncoordinated."

"No-o-o," he agreed, turning her hand over in his. "I like watching you move."

She blushed at the intimate sound in his voice. His color seemed to be returning. She'd better concentrate on his health and ignore her quickening heartbeat.

"That doesn't mean I'm going to let you go out in the dark and try a balancing act with an armful of logs on an icy path you aren't familiar with. We'll manage." He grinned. "And there are vicious trees about, remember?"

He absently traced the lines on her palm with his finger. Icy flames danced along her spine and she jerked her hand away, stretching to explain her sudden movement. "At least it's warm in here now," she said. "And I can get the two blankets off the bed in the other room. That should help us get through the night without more wood."

"We'll add one log at a time when the fire's almost gone." Matt yawned.

Were his pupils dilated? She felt helpless again. What if she couldn't tell if he needed a doctor before it was too late to find a way to get one?

Matt sipped some of the broth she brought him, then slept. Jillian sat upright in a chair, resisting sleep. She woke him every two hours to check his pupils and see if he was lucid. The second time she brought him some aspirin for the mild headache he admitted having.

Around midnight, the second to the last log was rapidly becoming a smoldering ember, and she could see her breath. She considered turning on the oven but decided against it. It was something of a relic, and she feared it might gas them both while they slept.

When her fingers were numb from the cold, she unearthed the travel alarm she'd packed out of habit, setting it for 2:00 a.m. The bare essentials of getting ready for bed completed, she crawled under the layer of heavy blankets. She didn't worry about what Matt might think as she coiled herself against his back, reversing their positions of the previous night. Maybe with her hand over his heart, she'd notice any change in his condition. And if he commented about the way she "plastered" herself against him, she'd plead the cold.

Matt was his irritable self when she woke him at two. He watched as she unsuccessfully attempted to relight the fire. Eventually he got out of bed to do it, despite her protests. He used the last log, closed the damper as far as he possibly could and raised crossed fingers as she held up the covers for him to get back onto bed. "I guess we're on our own when that one's gone." His eyes glittered wickedly as he leaned toward her and planted a quick kiss on her mouth. "Think we can generate some heat?"

Her eyelids drooped and her body screamed, "Danger." "I'm going back to sleep," she said, turning away from him.

"Shall we cuddle your way, this time?" he murmured, nestling into her. Jillian pretended to be already asleep.

The alarm went off at four. Matt lay on his back with his arm circling her. Her head was on his chest. Jillian propped herself on her elbow and shook him gently. "What?' he groaned irritably.

"Wake up."

"I'm awake, Jillian. Please, leave me alone."

Well, at least he knew her name. She leaned across him to light the lantern. It was on the coffee table she'd pulled over next to the bed. "What time is it?" she asked, hoping he'd open his eyes to look at his watch. She wanted to check them.

"Who cares?" he moaned, defeating her plan. He turned onto his side and pressed deeper into his pillow.

"Wake up, Matt." She laid a hand on his shoulder to prod him.

Suddenly, he was sitting. "I've been awake for hours," he flared. Grasping her arms, he reversed their positions so quickly that she found herself flat on her back and staring up at him, wide-eyed with surprise. He was leaning over her. "I think you want to leave me alone, Jillian."

For a moment, she forgot her reason for bothering him. Her lips went dry as his eyes lingered on her mouth.

"How much do you expect me to take? Every time I get to sleep, you wake me up and turn me on like a light. Then you roll over and go to sleep." His head dipped closer to hers. "Even Grandma wouldn't expect me to endure this without some return." His lips made gentle contact as his hand wandered down her side.

"Matt," she protested against his mouth, "I woke you to make sure you're all right."

"I'm fine, Jake. Never been better." His fingers fumbled with the knit edging of her sweatshirt, then he slid his hand under it and onto bare skin. Her stomach lurched.

"Matt," she tried to protest again, but the way she sighed his name sounded more like an invitation.

He lifted his head. "If I have a concussion, it's a slight one," he said in a voice that told her just how good he felt. "Why do you think I fell in the first place?" He continued to stroke her midriff. She couldn't have responded if her life depended on it.

"I wasn't thinking about what I was doing," he continued, answering his own question. "I was thinking about you."

The look in his eyes was doing funny things to her. "I want to make love to you," he whispered.

Her lips quivered in the attempt to say something—anything.

"Why do you think I stayed out in the cold all day? I was fighting the urge to do this." He bent to sprinkle mind-reeling kisses from her lips to a sensitive spot behind her ear. "Jillian, you're making me crazy."

His hand shaped itself around her breast. "Matt, this isn't the way it should be," she protested feebly, aching to give in to her body's demands, but trying to be sensible.

"How should it be? I want you...." His lips covered hers as if he could hold back any disagreement. "And I think you want me, too. Stop me if I'm wrong."

CHAPTER SIX

HIS SWEET KISSES turned hungry. Jillian's hands involuntarily wrapped around his shoulders and she pulled him closer, needing him, longing for release from the intense pressures building within her.

Her lips felt desperate for more. She parted them in invitation and his mouth explored hers searchingly. She found the taste of him delightful.

He broke off the kiss to trace the shell of her ear with his tongue. She giggled softly. "That tickles," she whispered, unaware of the way her body arched against his.

His hands were skillfully leading her to the point of delirium. He dropped a kiss on her eager lips then pressed his full length against her.

One of her hands weaved its way through his hair and the other slid beneath his shirt. She stroked his heated skin. Moving against him, she was shyly conscious of the intimacy of their touch, yet aching with need.

"You're beautiful," he murmured against her silky neck. His words sent a shiver of desire from her toes to her fingertips and back again.

His hands renewed their exploration of her body. "You're so beautiful, Jillian," he echoed breathlessly, "so lovely. Do you know what you do to me?" Her hands flattened against his back and held him close.

A tide of emotions surged through her and her heart thundered until she thought it would burst. "I love you," she whispered against his ear, putting a name to her feelings and leaving a kiss with her words.

His fingers drifted to a stop across the flat of her stomach. "Are you protected?" he asked huskily, lifting himself away from her and allowing the cold to rush in at her.

Jillian blinked, not understanding. Her eyes glazed with confusion.

He lowered his head to nibble briefly at her neck. "Are you protected?" he repeated.

Jillian's mind worked frantically as her body lay motionless. She was stunned by the sudden intrusion of reality. "No!" she managed to gasp, protesting their mutual insanity.

He raised an eyebrow in surprise and rolled away from her. "I assumed that since you were meeting the boyfriend..." He let the rest of the statement drift away and started to leave the now bone-jarringly cold bed. "Don't worry. I'll take care of it."

"Matt?" She gulped back a sob.

He paused in the act of taking off his heavy shirt. Goose bumps rose along his bare back, and her fingers itched to smooth them away, itched to touch him again.

"Yes?" His passion-heavy eyes examined her body.

She couldn't speak. Feeling exposed and vulnerable despite her sweat suit, she drew up the blanket to screen herself from his gaze.

"It's nothing to worry about," he assured her. "I'll be back in a minute."

"No." She locked her eyes on the dark ceiling, guilt-ridden over what her instincts had led him to expect, ashamed that she didn't want to stop even now.

He leaned down and eased a lock of hair from her face. "Two consenting adults don't *have* to declare love before they make love," he explained gently, referring to the declaration she had made from her heart only moments before. She wished he hadn't heard it. "We *do* have an obligation to prevent an unwanted pregnancy. I wouldn't do that to you, Jake. Think what *that* would do to your dreams of playing house and living happily ever after."

He started to kiss her and she turned her head. The heart that had raced in response to his burst into a million tiny pieces and she crumbled inside from the pain. "I didn't mean 'no, I'm not protected.' I meant 'no, I can't do this,'" she whispered between parched lips. "It's all wrong. I…we…" She couldn't meet his intent eyes. "Long after I've forgotten the effect you've had on me tonight—" *I'll never forget,* she realized "—I'll regret this," she finished miserably.

"Sometimes you take what fate hands you and don't worry about what will happen next. This feels right, doesn't it?" Matt's hand cupped the side of her face and Jillian leaned into it, like a kitten seeking a stroke. "You're feeling guilt about the boyfriend? He doesn't own you," he added, urging her to grant him the same rights she had intended to grant Harrison.

"I plan to spend the rest of my life with him," she defended herself.

He said nothing—didn't move—just braced himself on his hands above her and questioned her decision with puzzled eyes. "You want me," he stated in a cool, factual tone that made her shiver.

She didn't deny the truth, but tried to control the shakiness in her voice. "You said that two consenting adults didn't have to profess love, but I want someone who *does* love me. I can't ignore the promises I've made to Harrison, disregarding everything I've always dreamed of, simply because my body is in control instead of my brain. You were right. One night could change everything."

His jaw tightened. A vein throbbed in his neck. "There *are* no lifetime guarantees."

"I know." A choking sadness closed her throat. "But I've never been one to casually give myself away in bits and pieces."

"I didn't think you were."

"Would you want me to sleep around if I was your fiancée?"

"If you were my fiancée—" He broke off, wrenching away from her and out of the bed. "Damn. You've got me talking like I believe in your fairy tales."

"I'm sorry. I shouldn't have let things get out of hand. I wasn't—I couldn't think." She forced herself to speak calmly. Putting on a good act was everything now. In his memories, she wanted to be the sophisticated woman-who-got-away, not a prehistoric frightened virgin who couldn't cope with her feelings for him. Tapping her forehead in the same general vicinity as his bandage, she ended the discussion. "I'm sure this isn't doing your head any good."

Holding the covers close to her breasts, she lifted his side of the blankets. "Now, you'd better get back in bed before you freeze to death."

Matt's eyes widened in disbelief, then without a word, he yanked his insulated shirt over his head and strode to the bathroom.

Jillian carefully refrained from looking after him. With a shudder that felt as if it came from her soul, she slid down beneath the covers to quietly lick her wounds.

She was so disgusted with herself, it took an effort not to cry. She wanted him—with every aching pulse point in her body. Desire was something she'd never really experienced before—she didn't know how to deal with it. But how could she have mistaken desire for love?

Matt didn't have any such problem. He wanted a casual roll in the hay. At the mention of the word *love*, he thought of protection. Did she want to give her whole self—heart, body and soul—to someone who wanted only safe little fragments? And if she gave her body to Matt, how would she piece herself back together for Harrison?

Did she want to?

She cared for Harrison. He shared her vision of the future. He kept loneliness away. Did that add up to love? No, she admitted, and pain knotted her stomach.

She'd always believed her reluctance to sleep with Harrison was a result of Grandma's straitlaced teachings. Maybe that had been part of it, but her feelings, or lack thereof, explained a lot.

So why this outrageous longing for Matt?

Jillian stiffened as she heard him come back and pretended to be asleep. He wasn't fooled, but it was easier for both of them this way. He stayed far over on his side of the bed, his back to her. She stayed on hers.

Her eyes burned from not crying, her body ached from stiffly holding herself away from him and trying to keep her teeth from chattering. Dawn was sneaking around the edges of the curtains before she finally let herself relax enough to fall asleep.

"WHAT the hell?"

Harrison's voice jarred Jillian awake. As she groped for words to explain the apparently compromising situation, Harrison's jaw sagged, and Matt calmly got out of the bed and told him the truth—or at least most of it.

"You must be Harry," Matt finished in his easy drawl, though his chin was set and rigid.

Harrison scowled. "The name is Harrison." The tall, model-thin man looked down his nose at Matt.

Jillian watched as Matt's fist clenched. A punch in the mouth wouldn't help matters, she decided, and quickly rose to her knees, pulling the blankets with her.

Harrison turned his sanctimonious stare on her.

"It isn't the way it looks, Harrison—"

Matt cut her off. "You don't owe him any explanation, Jake." He kept his eyes trained on the new arrival. "He should have been here if he wanted a say in what happened."

Harrison's expression darkened.

"Nothing happened," she denied quickly, as much to Matt as to Harrison.

"She's right," Matt agreed derisively, snatching his jeans from the back of the couch. "Nothing except being snowed in without electricity or heat or a phone."

With characteristic grace, Matt yanked the jeans on over his long underwear and Jillian realized that Harrison's suspicions were justified. Three days ago, she would have hidden her face in the blanket, uncomfortable that Matt was dressing in front of her. Now, she watched unself-consciously.

Matt sat down on the edge of the bed and viciously pulled his boots on. His stark white bandage clashed with his angry red face, reminding her that he shouldn't even *be* out of bed. Not till he'd seen a doctor.

"How did you get here, Harrison?" Jillian demanded, her question surprising both men. "Can we get out now? Matt needs to see a doctor."

"Dammit, Jillian, I don't need a doctor." Matt grabbed his still-damp ski jacket, then exchanged it for his dry coat. "You'd better straighten out your boyfriend before I do," he warned her, then slammed out of the cabin before either of them could say another word.

Jillian took a deep breath and chanced a look up at Harrison. His face could have been chiseled out of stone. "So?" he demanded, compressing his thin lips into a grim line.

I have to tell him I can't marry him. What a ludicrous thought! All she really had to do was let him continue to think what he was thinking. "Let me get dressed, Harrison. Then we can talk." She was stalling for time, but how could she say what she needed to without some preparation?

He nodded, granting her the permission she realized she didn't need. With the blanket wrapped around her, she headed toward the bedroom. It occurred to her only after she closed the door that she was fully clothed in her jogging suit.

When she returned, Harrison was sitting stiffly in a chair next to the dead fire. "Now," she began, speaking in her most reasonable voice, and sinking onto the pullout bed. "Did you hear me tell you about Matt before we were cut off on Christmas Eve."

Harrison looked at her blankly.

"He arrived shortly before you called." She filled the gaps in Matt's earlier explanation, but left out the important things—the playful fight in the snow, the way Matt had comforted her when she'd cried.... Christmas Day seemed like a story from the distant past. Her hand went automatically to the necklace Matt had given her. The bells' small lump beneath her heavy sweater made it all real again.

Of course, she didn't mention the terror she'd felt when she found Matt lying in the snow, or the way her body reacted when he touched her. But when Harrison reached for her hand and began telling her how anxious he'd been for them to be together, she drew away.

"What's the matter?" he asked plaintively. She suddenly recognized that he'd always sounded like that; she'd simply never noticed it before.

"Things have changed," Jillian said fixedly. "Since I've been here I've realized we don't feel the way two people who plan to be married should."

"I haven't changed," he protested. "I still want to marry you."

She smiled wryly. Harrison didn't normally make concessions when things didn't go his way. "Maybe more so now than before?"

"What do you mean?" he asked, raising an aristocratic brow.

"This is the most enthusiastic I've seen you since we began talking about marriage. Let's face it, the subject only came up after I repeatedly refused to go to bed with you." She stared at her ringless hand, remembering his vague proposal. "If you really loved me, Harrison, why didn't you want to introduce me to your family? We've been seeing each other on and off for almost two years." He would have interrupted but she stopped him with an upflung hand. "Why did you suddenly decide we should become engaged? Was it because you wanted to come here to. . .celebrate?"

"Jillian, I—"

"It seems to me that you were a lot more interested in the honeymoon than the marriage. And you weren't even too concerned about *that* or you wouldn't have let me get snowed in here by myself Christmas Eve."

"You're going to hold that against me? You don't seem to realize I have obligations—"

"Exactly. And some of them ought to be to your family." Jillian lifted her head. "If you really loved me, you'd want me to feel *part* of your family. But that's beside the point," she added quietly, slipping her hands beneath her thighs. "I've been so busy telling myself how nicely you'd fill in all the blanks in my life—especially since Grandma died—that I forgot what's really important to me."

Harrison didn't say anything for a long moment, and Jillian scuffed her foot against a braid in the circular rug covering the floor.

"What has all of this got to do with *him*?" Harrison tossed his head in the direction of the back door, his thick, carefully styled hair remaining stiffly in place. He could have posed for a paper doll of the perfect husband, she realized, half-fascinated, half-mortified by her newfound perceptions.

How often had he called to cancel their plans because he had to work late? If she'd married him, nothing would have changed. The ambition that had drawn her to him would have kept him working long hours, and she'd have raised their children alone.

It wasn't all his fault, she admitted. She'd admired his dedication and been thankful that she didn't have to fight him off. She'd been content to be "window dressing." She'd even fantasized about being the perfect little wife, entertaining his associates and helping him further his political ambitions.

"Why do I suspect that things would still be as we planned if he wasn't involved? Did you sleep with him?"

She blushed. "Not the way you mean." He was watching her carefully and she looked away.

"Then I don't see what the problem is, Jillian. I trust you. If you wouldn't with me—"

"That's not the point," she said impatiently.

"What is?"

"I don't love you."

Harrison mulled that over for a moment, his expression blank. "Then it does have something to do with him."

"No," she replied wearily.

"Then why have you decided we aren't compatible when you've never questioned it before?"

Finally, a question that was easy. "Because of Christmas. Because you didn't come."

"I see." His lips twisted into a smug smile. "This is retribution for my not being here Christmas Eve."

Jillian shook her head.

"You're being impetuous, you know."

"I was being impetuous when I agreed to come here with you. What I wanted more than anything was to share Christmas with you and your family."

Harrison didn't comment, and the silence between them stretched uncomfortably.

"I'm sorry, Harrison. I convinced myself that we wanted the same things, but things that are important to me don't mean anything to you." She met his brown eyes, steadily.

"Such as?"

"Your family, Harrison. You don't spend any time with them. Would you have time for our own family if we were married?"

Harrison set his mouth in a thin, straight line. "I'm at a crucial point in my career. It's important that I establish the right contacts now. I thought you understood that, Jillian."

Jillian turned away. "I think I do," she responded sadly.

"So I'm expected to wait around until you change your mind?"

"Please, Harrison, let's just go back to being friends?"

Harrison rose, pulling her up with him. "I'm sure you'll come to your senses, but don't wait too long. I can see I've been too patient with you."

Jillian ducked his outstretched arm and moved out of reach.

He shook his head and picked up his neatly folded coat. "I'm going back to civilization," he stated, looking around him disdainfully. "You know where to find me."

Jillian didn't move. She heard his car start and slowly navigate the lane.

She was still standing there when Matt came in with an armful of logs and bent to place them neatly across the cold, dark embers in the fireplace. "What happened?" he asked casually, and became very busy building a fire.

She felt emotionally drained and shrugged listlessly. His back was still to her so she added, "It doesn't matter." Last night and the unpleasant scene that had finished only moments before combined to add an unhappy sigh to the last word. She didn't notice that Matt had come to stand in front of her until he lifted her chin and looked carefully into her eyes. They immediately filled with tears.

He groaned. "Your happiness matters. I take it Harry didn't believe what you told him. If it would help," he offered, "I'll explain—"

Jillian blinked away the moisture clouding her vision. "There's nothing to explain," she interrupted and backed away leaving his hand in the air.

"Things have a way of working themselves out. He'll understand when he's had time to think about it. I almost wish . . ."

Jillian waited for him to finish his thought, but he didn't. "If wishes were horses, we wouldn't have been stuck here." Her attempt at flippancy sounded forced and humorless.

"What are you going to do now?"

"Pack." Jillian followed the word with the action.

Matt trailed after her into the kitchen where she opened the door of the utility closet and pulled out several of the boxes she'd stashed there. He lingered silently as she went to the Christmas tree and began removing ornaments, placing them gently in the box.

"I didn't mean 'now,' this instant. I meant 'now,' from this moment on."

She didn't answer. Discussing her future with a man who immediately thought of birth control when the word *love* was mentioned seemed pointless. She had one of the small ornament boxes filled before he continued.

"You shouldn't... I don't think..." He cleared his throat. "Don't rush things."

Jillian turned on him. "What are you suggesting I do? Spit it out, Matt."

He took the box from her and set it on the table.

"I just don't want you to be upset or hurt." He lightly caressed her arms, then pulled her close. So close that if she took a deep breath she'd brush against his chest.

His whole attitude made her angry. It wasn't his dreams that had just gone down the drain. But it wasn't his fault, she reminded herself. She'd chosen to break her engagement to Harrison. She counted to ten. "I'll get over it."

"I don't like seeing a friend unhappy." One hand left her arm and he stroked her hair gently, his fingers lingering against her neck.

Friends? So *that* was what they were. "I'll live." She shrugged away from his touch. "Men! I'm about to decide I'm nuts for ever thinking I wanted one." She pulled out another box and resumed dismantling the tree.

"Jillian?" He sounded perplexed.

"Please. I'd appreciate it if you'd just leave me alone."

"You need time to put things into perspective. You should stay. You don't have to leave."

"No," she agreed, "but my reason for being here no longer exists."

Jillian sensed Matt's reluctance to drop the subject but managed to treat him like a piece of the furniture as he followed her around. He finally offered to fix them a light brunch while she finished taking decorations off the Christmas tree.

When Matt announced the meal, she sat down at the table and he handed her a bowl of fresh-from-the-can peaches. "About last night—"

"Please, Matt, I don't want to talk about it."

"Harrison's reaction—"

"That either," she interrupted again. He sighed and ate. Jillian endured the strained silence, punctuated only by the clatter of forks against plates as long as she could before asking, somewhat mockingly, "Now that my plans are taken care of, what are your plans?"

"I'll be going back to Topeka for a few days when I leave here."

"Oh?" She couldn't think of anything else to say. The questions she wanted to ask—did he ever get lonely? Did he have someone special anywhere? Did he have women waiting in every town between here and Denver?—didn't seem appropriate.

"I've got some business to take care of with Jim. Besides being my friend, he's my accountant, if you hadn't guessed. We grew up in the same town."

If Jillian was surprised, it was because he'd offered information without a full-scale probing operation. "Where is home now?" She spoke casually, telling herself she really didn't care, that anything was better than cold silence.

"Colorado, I guess."

"Is that your main office? How do you manage to run all your stores from a distance?" Nice safe topic, she thought.

"I hire good management people."

It was as brief an answer as possible. So much for safe. He didn't want to discuss himself, and she didn't want to talk about her over-before-it-began engagement. "Good omelet," she complimented, finishing as much as she could choke down, then pushing her plate aside. "Thank you. You'll forgive me if I leave the dishes for you?" She started to rise to go back to her packing, but he stopped her by reviving the conversation she'd thought ended.

"It'll take several days with Jim to finish up the year-end reports before I leave Topeka. That's one of the reasons I came here instead of going to my sister's for Christmas. I didn't want to turn around and come right back." Matt pushed his chair away from the table. "I also have to decide whether I want to sell my stores," he threw out.

Something in the way he said it asked for comment, but she couldn't think of any. She tilted her head expectantly, encouraging him to elaborate.

"I've had a pretty good offer from a national chain." Matt planted his feet wide and rocked the chair back on two legs. "Think I should take it?"

She felt flattered that he'd asked her opinion, yet leery. "I don't know. Do you want to?"

He shrugged.

"What will you do if you sell?"

He hooked his fingers in the pockets of his worn jeans. "I don't know. I won't have to do anything if I accept."

"I can't picture you being very good at doing nothing."

He seemed tense as he leaned forward, elbows on knees. "You see my dilemma?"

She nodded.

"But on the other hand, the challenge is definitely gone. I'm tired of selling jewelry to rich old ladies and foolish young men."

His gaze came to rest on Jillian's bare hand and she tucked it under her thigh. "Give it away," she suggested cattily.

"The stores or the jewelry?"

She relaxed and smiled. "Both."

He threw back his head and laughed. "I'm going to miss you, Jake." A teasing light came into his eyes. "Sure you don't want to stay? We could work through our dilemmas together."

"I don't have a dilemma," she replied abruptly and rose to go back to work.

"I'll come by and see you before I leave Topeka." The comment could have been either a promise or a threat.

However he meant it, Jillian was sure it wouldn't help her peace of mind. "I don't think that's such a good idea."

"You're afraid I'll hamper your reconciliation with Harrison?"

She gave him a puzzled scowl.

"If you want me to fix things up..." She wasn't sure if the distaste in his voice was for Harrison or for the proposed reunion.

Did he think the scene with Harrison was just a little spat to be cleared up with the Christmas debris? She opened her mouth to tell him, point-blank, that there would be no reconciliation, then snapped it shut. She didn't have anything to gain by discussing further. "Don't worry about it."

"But I will," he insisted, adding, "I don't cheat on important things."

His grin faded at her blank frown.

"I cheated the other night when we played Scrabble," he admitted sheepishly.

Her shoulders sagged with the anticlimax. "What does that have to do with anything?"

He ignored the question, as usual. "Arg isn't a word. I made it up."

He took one of her hands in his, confusing and frustrating her. "Damn it, Matt." She shook her hand free.

"I didn't kno. you took the game so seriously." His eyes matched the mischievous grin that inevitably managed to charm her.

"Damn you, Matt Carson," she swore softly again. "Would you get to the point?"

"Even though *not* making love to you was the hardest thing I've ever done, we didn't really *do* anything."

Only because you were so concerned about "protecting" yourself that I had time to think about my own welfare, she thought resentfully.

"I don't want you to blame me for the way things worked out." Matt's jaw set in a hard line. "Frankly, I don't want you to make up with him—he was deplorable—but I can't let my personal opinions cheat you out of something you really want. If Harry is important to you, I'll talk to him."

Jillian watched his hand clench. Why the offer? He obviously detested the whole idea. Was she afraid she'd throw herself on the floor, wrap her arms around his knees and beg him to make an honest woman of her? If he'd been watching her eyes, he would have seen angry sparks in them. She knew why he was so anxious to "fix" things.

Jillian took another deep breath and counted to twenty. "Are you reminding me that nothing happened between us because you're afraid I'll expect something from you?"

He took one look at her and immediately moved out of firing range.

His nervousness would have been amusing if she hadn't felt like throwing something at him. "Just because you wanted to take Harrison's place in my bed, I don't expect you to step in now, okay?''

''I'm not good husband material—''

''Did you hear me say I thought you were?'' She should have got a little satisfaction from his protest, but got mad instead. ''You already warned me, Matt. Don't worry, I don't expect you to save my honor because Harrison mistakenly assumed you disgraced me.''

Matt reached toward her and she avoided him the same way she'd avoided Harrison earlier. ''Contrary to the way it may have seemed from time to time since we got here, I can handle my own life. Thanks, anyway.''

She shook her head as if ridding herself of a bad dream. It wasn't going to be hard to say goodbye to Matt after all, she decided. Who needed him? For years, she and Grandma had fared quite well without having a man around.

CHAPTER SEVEN

JILLIAN RETURNED to her packing.

Matt asked to borrow her car. "I'll run into town to see about getting the electricity and phone back in service," he explained.

Jillian reached for her purse and fished out her keys. "Get your head checked," she said succinctly, throwing them at him. Then she went back to her work.

When he returned, she was trying to drag the seven-foot, long-needled pine out the back door. "Why didn't you wait for me?" he asked, sounding exasperated. "Let me help."

"I'm quite capable," she answered and continued tugging. One of the branches seemed to be caught on something.

Matt moved her out of the way and grabbed the bedraggled thing by its trunk.

"I got it in by myself," she said defensively, stepping out of the way as he backed it through the door.

"Yeah, I wondered about that the night I got here." He carried the once beautiful tree to the edge of the clearing, then walked toward her, brushing loose needles from his clothes. "I wondered how you got it in the stand by yourself."

"An old trick Grandma and I perfected," she said enigmatically, refusing to meet his eyes, refusing to let their relationship revert to its earlier easy camaraderie. She swung around, head proudly aloft, to go back inside.

"You could thank me," Matt said.

"I didn't ask for your help." Jillian held the door, waiting for him to come in. "I could have done it."

"You don't need *help*, Jake," he said, compressing his lips tightly. "You need a guardian."

"I've got one, a guardian angel, remember?"

Matt gave her one last frown, turned and stalked down the path she'd hauled him up the evening before. "I'm going to replenish the woodpile," he called gruffly before disappearing among the trees.

"I don't need your agenda," she mumbled, then remembered what had happened last night and fought the urge to tell him to report in regularly. Instead, she paused in her work from time to time and watched him.

Once, Matt glanced up and saw her at the window. He started toward the cabin, then hesitated. She quickly moved away.

It was almost three o'clock when he placed the last logs on the stack of wood that had been growing outside the back door and came in.

"Looks like you're almost done," he said, glancing at her pile of things by the front door.

"I need to leave soon. If I get home by five, I won't have to unload all this after dark." She looked at him—*really* looked at him for the first time all day, and realized he was slightly pale. "Did you see a doctor while you were in Pomona?"

He shook his head. "I'll get it looked at when I get back home," he promised.

"I'd better change that bandage before I go," she said and went for the first-aid kit. She expected an argument as she sat down at the kitchen table and laid out the supplies. He surprised her by meekly obeying her somewhat gruff orders.

"How's it feeling?" She gently peeled away the previous bandage.

"Okay, I guess."

"It looks nasty," she said grimacing.

He chuckled. "That bad?" His eyes met hers and she wavered. He steadied her by putting his hands on her waist, then pulled her to stand between his knees.

As irritated as she'd been with him most of the day, he still had a wild effect on her pulses. She held herself stiffly to keep her legs from coming in contact with his.

"You need stitches," she forced herself to say calmly. In a couple of hours, she wouldn't have to cope with these erratic and unexpected sensations.

Her breast brushed his shoulders and he drew a sharp breath. Circling her wrists with his hands, he held them away from him as if he found her touch agonizing. She marveled that she had the same electrifying effect on him.

"Jillian, if you'd like to stay, I'll leave if you want me to. The power should be on soon and they promised to get the phone fixed before dark."

She softened—slightly. "Thanks for the thought, Matt, but I've got a lot of things I need to do anyway. It would be nice to start the new year with a clean slate."

"Jillian?"

She waited. She wanted to hear what he had to say so much that she trembled.

"Damn," Matt cursed, steadying her a second time. He dropped his hand quickly and she swayed again.

"Damn," he repeated, standing and folding her in his arms. "Surely I deserve one small remembrance, sweet Jillian." His arms tightened as she leaned into his strength. His lips drew closer, and her body became fluid and weak with anticipation.

Oh, Matt, she moaned silently. A thought hit her in the pit of her stomach. If she saw him again, he'd be a casual acquaintance. He'd never call her Jake in that tender way. He'd never touch her and make her pulses race. She studied his face carefully, feature by feature. His heated look stopped her heart and her lips rose longingly to his.

He pushed her away, jamming his hands into the pockets of his heavy cords. "I didn't intend to do that," he said, sinking back into the chair.

Jillian felt numb as she watched his square jaw harden and his eyes turn cold. "No problem," she croaked, stepping out of Matt's sensory range to reach for the bandage she'd put on the table. "I'm sure you didn't." She didn't know whether her gasps for air were caused by frustration, confusion or his continued closeness. Maybe she should stay. From the beginning, his reaction to her had been as reckless as her reaction to him. The attraction was definitely mutual. Could they build something from that? Lord knew she wanted to. But—and the "but" was a big one—could they ever meet each other's needs when she wanted the moon and the stars and he wanted nothing? He *had* graduated from "not being the mar-

rying kind" to "not being good husband material,"
she thought wryly. Was that progress?

She finished her task, careful to avoid touching any
part of him but his forehead. "There," she said, putting the last piece of adhesive in place. "I guess I'll get
the rest of my stuff into the car." She forced herself to
concentrate on the task at hand. Keys. Coat.

"Here, let me help you with that." Matt carried out
the largest box and set it on the hood of the car. Ex-
tricating the car keys from her fingers and opening the
trunk, he took the box she was holding and placed it
inside. She headed back to the cabin for more just as
the phone rang.

"Sounds like they got it fixed. They're probably
checking the line. You answer it and I'll finish loading everything for you," Matt offered.

"I'll get the bags in the bedroom," she called as she
hurried in.

By the time she finished the conversation, the rest
of her things were stowed away and Matt was adding
marshmallows to hot chocolate. "I thought you might
need a little sustenance for the trip," he explained,
handing her a mug. He obviously wasn't anxious for
her to leave.

"It's cold, but it's sunny. Let's sit out on the back
porch."

"The man on the phone was the one you talked to
about getting your Blazer out of the ditch." She re-
layed the message as he grabbed his coat from the
hook. "He said that a farmer who lives not too far
from here is coming over when he finishes his chores."

"Good." He opened the door for them.

He sat down on the top step and raised his arm, inviting her to sit under the warmth of it. She hesitated only a fraction of a second before accepting the invitation. What could it hurt? She'd be gone in another five minutes. Steam rose from the stoneware mugs as he wrapped his arm around her shoulders and pulled her against him.

She sat solemnly, savoring this final bit of sharing. It felt completely natural to be close to him, even though they'd been at odds most of the day.

Matt cleared his throat. "I do care what happens to you, Jake."

She gazed up at him, her eyes wide. He stared hard at the sparkling landscape in front of them. "I know." It took an incredible effort, but she managed to keep her voice even.

Surprisingly enough, she *did* know he cared for her, and the knowledge comforted and scared her. Jillian's heart thudded heavily.

"Are you going to make up with him?" he asked quietly, removing his sheltering arm from her shoulders. "Marriage is supposed to be forever. That's a long time."

"You're right about that," she agreed. It was easy to discuss theory, since there wasn't going to be a marriage, to Harrison or anyone else, for a long, long time.

The desire to get married and settle down had been only a vague dream until Grandma died. After that it became a gnawing hunger. She wanted someone of her own—but you couldn't go around marrying just anyone simply because you didn't want to be alone.

And she didn't intend to compound her problem by spending too much time with a dyed-in-the-wool loner who made her toes curl whenever he looked at her.

"I don't want you to make a mistake," he continued.

"You said there wasn't such a thing as happily-ever-after, so if I marry *anyone*, you'd consider it a mistake, right?"

"Maybe I was wrong." Matt held her eyes with his.

Jillian closed hers, breaking the contact. "It doesn't matter, Matt."

He touched her hand. "There are other men, better—"

"It's irrelevant," she interrupted. "I'm not going to marry him." She wished she didn't feel like crying; she wished she could attribute the tears to Harrison.

He leaned back, stretching his arms above his head.

For a moment, she hated him. He didn't want her, but he sure as heck didn't like the idea of Harrison having her, either. So, now he could relax.

He took her empty cup and set it on the railing. Pulling her to her feet as he rose, he turned her to face him. His hazel eyes seemed a brilliant green as they studied hers. They sparked with an inner fire, and the slight wind ruffled his ash-blond hair. "Can I see you when I'm in Topeka?"

He *did* want her. The wanting was in every hungry line of his body. It was in his eyes. Obviously, he believed it was only a matter of time. Her mouth quivered as his head drew steadily closer, her lips parted involuntarily. If her heart had pounded any harder she'd probably have passed out. And yet nothing had changed—it was the same old impossible situation.

Although he wanted her as much as she wanted him, he didn't want any part of the commitment that she believed went with the wanting. She turned her head away, when his mouth would have touched hers. His kiss glanced off her cheek instead. "I'm not going to have an affair with you, if that's what you think," she denied huskily.

His hand curved around the nape of her neck, catching strands of her wind-scattered hair. He drew her to him and placed a gentle kiss on her forehead, then held her close, her head nestled into the curve of his neck.

She knew she should move, put some distance between them, but she couldn't.

"I'm not asking you to have an affair with me," he said quietly.

They stood, unmoving, for a time measured only in heartbeats. "It's getting very cold out here." The chill was settling into her very soul. Could she handle friendship with Matt? No.

"I need to be off." She tried to move away.

Matt tightened his hold. "Why were you going to let me make love to you, Jillian?"

She looked up at him warily. Did his outsize ego need her to reiterate that she loved him, so he could turn away in rejection again? "Because, like the mountain, you were there." She pulled out of his arms. "I'm going now, before I freeze to death." She glanced at her watch. "The farmer who's going to pull your car out of the ditch should be here soon."

"I'll walk you out." He slipped inside with the mugs and grabbed her purse from the counter. "Come on." He handed her the purse.

"Surely I deserve one small remembrance," he'd said earlier. Her hands grew clammy waiting for him to take it. Against all common sense she wanted to feel his lips on hers once more. Just once. Yet she was reluctant to look at him. She was afraid she'd wrap herself around him, begging him to make love to her so she *could* expect him to make an honest woman of her. Okay, she'd have an affair with him.... No. They'd hate each other within six months and she'd be back where she'd started, alone and looking for anything and anyone to fill the void. And she'd never have the kind of life she longed for, the kind of life she needed. Matt was dangerous. He could start a whole disastrous cycle.

They walked to her car in silence. Putting his hand to the small of her back, he helped her in, treating her as if she were somehow fragile.

The door closed with a sound of finality and she rolled down the window.

Matt crossed his arms and leaned in.

"Well, thanks for everything," she said ruefully. "You've taken care of me every bit as well as Grandma could have wanted."

He gave her a sideways glance and smiled. His silky mustache angled devilishly. "Don't tell anyone. My reputation will be shot."

As if he couldn't resist, he reached in to tweak her nose. "It's been ... interesting," he said with a rasp.

Jillian turned the ignition, swallowing hard to get rid of the persistent lump in her throat. *Don't embarrass yourself,* she willed, looking over her shoulder to check the path. She put the little car into gear. "Bye,

Matt," she said softly, allowing herself one more long look at him.

"See you." His "see you" was a promise. She could see the determined glint in his eyes.

"No, Matt. Please don't look me up. It wouldn't serve any purpose and you could hurt me a lot."

Matt seemed startled that she'd put it into words.

"Bye, Matt," she repeated.

He started to say something but she released the brake and backed out of his life.

JILLIAN WAS HALFWAY to Topeka when the numbness wore off. An ache spread in her chest. She suddenly felt weary—and more alone than she had ever felt. First Grandma. Then Harrison. Now Matt. The names became a litany.

By the time she turned her car into the parking space in front of her apartment, Jillian was sick of thinking about the past. Somehow she had to get her life back on track. No more disasters like Harrison. No more instant emotional attachments to whoever happened to be handy, she vowed, then realized she'd just put a three-day acquaintance in the same category as her former almost-fiancé.

She mentally checked her bank balance as she unloaded the car. Money was definitely a problem if she decided to make any major changes in her life.

She'd gone to work for the senator as soon as she'd graduated from secretarial school. Grandma had known him when he was a boy in their hometown. And Grandma figured the big city wasn't as much of a threat if Jillian was under the protection of someone important.

It was a good job and she'd been content until now. But there wasn't any future in it. Could she happily grow old managing the office? The very thought made the future seem terribly bleak. And Karen would be quitting at the end of the school year.

Jillian made one last trip to the car, locked it, then went back up to the apartment and fell into bed. But she didn't sleep.

She supposed she could take some night classes at the college. But what would she study? Music? She tried to visualize herself as a music teacher. The picture wouldn't come into focus.

Maybe she'd been too hasty in burning her bridges with Harrison. But *nothing* about that brief thought struck a chord. It was strange how easily she'd excised him from her plans. She'd really believed she cared for him, yet now that he was relegated to the past, he seemed to fit there better than he had ever fit into her future.

A deep quiet settled over the apartment. Not even the refrigerator hummed. She could have been the only person left on the planet. Alone in the dark, with her eyes wide open, she ached for a life that included people she loved.

No matter how many times she'd faced the fact that, someday, everyone had to die, she'd never believed Grandma would desert her. Even now, in the picture that wouldn't be banished from her mind, Grandma was firmly ensconced in the rocking chair in the center of her future, holding one great-grandchild on her knee, crooning softly to the sandy-headed toddler playing by her side.

Jillian let the familiar dream-movie run in her head. "Here, Grandma, you must be tired. Let me put the children to bed."

Grandma smiled as she gave up her burden.

"I'll get this one, Jake." A new presence intruded on her fantasy. And even in the dazed state between daydream and sleep Jillian's head jerked toward the familiar voice.

Matt grinned at her as he stepped forward and slung the laughing, delighted child over his shoulder.

Jillian moaned and shook her head to rid herself of the vision. She should have recognized the child. He was an exact miniature of the man. But Matt was as much a part of the past as Grandma and Harrison. She had to start thinking of him that way or not think of him at all.

"Oh, what am I going to do now?" she whispered to the empty room. A tear welled in her eye and she concentrated on the feel of it trickling down her cheek. "I can't be in love with him, can I, Grandma?" She turned over and buried her face in the pillow to shut out dreams that could never be.

"COME ON, JILLIAN."

The pounding on the door startled Jillian out of sleep, and she opened her eyes to a roomful of bright sunshine. She groggily got out of bed.

"Jillian? Your car is out there. I know you're—"

Karen almost fell in as Jillian opened the door.

"You were knocking loud enough to wake the dead, Karen. What time is it anyway?" Jillian hid a yawn behind her hand and rubbed her eyes. Turning her back and heading for the kitchen, she tacitly invited Karen to join her.

"It's almost nine. Well?" Karen demanded, closing the door and following. "What happened?"

"Let me wake up, for Pete's sake. You want some coffee?"

Karen nodded. "So why are you back?"

Jillian didn't answer until she'd flipped the switch on the coffee maker. It had been a long night and the daylight filtering through the kitchen blinds didn't seem to be doing much to clear her head.

"You weren't supposed to be back for another four days. You should have called." Karen's voice held a mixture of censure and worry.

"I didn't think you'd know I was back."

"Matt called."

Jillian suddenly felt wide awake. "I'm sorry. By the time I unpacked the car, I was so tired, I decided calling could wait until this morning since I wasn't supposed to be home anyway." She reached for her purse and concentrated on opening the outside pocket. "Matt called?"

"He wanted to make sure you made it back okay. He offered to phone you himself, but you know me. I couldn't wait to get the lowdown, so I told him I'd check on you. Then all I got was your damn answering machine, so I figured he'd misunderstood, and you and Harrison had gone off somewhere." She halted expectantly.

Jillian found the keys she'd been digging for and handed them to Karen. "Here. I appreciated the use of the cabin," she said lightly, "even if things didn't quite work as planned. As a matter of fact, Harrison didn't make it down until yesterday. Then he was only there for maybe an hour. We decided marriage wasn't such a good idea and he left.''

Karen's mouth dropped open, and Jillian had the unique pleasure of seeing her speechless. She sank into a chair. "You're kidding! Things didn't quite work out as planned?" Karen echoed. "What a massive understatement." Then her startled expression melted into one of understanding. "Ohh." She looked irritatingly smug. "You fell for Matt," she said knowingly. "You can't say I didn't warn you. Come on. Tell all. You can leave out the X-rated parts."

A lot of help Karen was. Jillian was trying to get things in their proper perspective and her best friend was making a big deal out of them. Jillian willed herself to reply casually, "What X-rated parts? Nothing happened." Thank heaven she could still say nothing happened, although it had been a near thing the night Matt got hurt.

"Sure. Sure. Nothing happened. The very thought of all that 'nothing' makes you blush—oh, yes, you are, Jilly," Karen said, stopping Jillian's protest. "So don't think you'll get out of telling me what went on." She followed Jillian to the coffee maker and propped herself against the counter as Jillian poured them each a cup.

Jillian had no idea what to tell her, so she silently waited for Karen's talking impulse to kick in and take over. She could then listen, making appropriate "ahs" and "uhms," and Karen wouldn't even realize that Jillian had said absolutely nothing.

"Come on, I'm not going to say another word until you tell me all about it," Karen told her as if reading Jillian's mind.

"What did Matt say when he called?" Jillian asked, buying time.

"Just that the roads still weren't totally clear and he wanted to make sure you'd made it home without any trouble. Your turn."

Jillian raised her shoulders, "I don't *know* what happened. How can I tell you?"

"For starters, you could explain why you aren't wearing a knockout engagement ring. What happened with Harrison? I thought making it official was the whole point of your secluded little celebration."

They had drifted back to the table and Jillian gave up fighting the inevitable. Maybe Karen would be able to make sense of the whole wretched business. She sketchily filled in what had happened between the time they'd talked on Christmas Eve and yesterday morning. "Then Harrison arrived and found me—innocently," she inserted quickly, "in bed with Matt. Needless to say, that was the end of the engagement."

Karen's jaw dropped a second time, and Jillian smiled. "I suppose you know the electricity was off for most of the time we were there?"

Karen nodded silently.

"Well, with no heat in the bedroom, Matt—gentleman that he is—informed me that I could sleep on the cold, hard floor or join him in the sofa bed. I didn't have any choice."

Now Karen laughed in sheer astonishment. "And nothing happened?"

"Nothing happened." If she said it often enough, maybe she'd convince herself. Because something *had* happened. Everything seemed slightly out of whack, as if nothing would ever be normal again.

"Matt must be slipping. What a jolt to his ego," Karen said finally. "I'll bet he feels like he's been hit by a Mack truck."

"He looks like it. He had a run-in with a very vicious tree." Jillian's tone was dry. "Did he happen to say if he'd been to see a doctor yet? He needs stitches."

Karen brushed aside that topic with a shake of her head. "He must have tried *something*."

"Well..." Jillian hesitated momentarily and decided to tell Karen everything. "Actually, I came close to...to..."

"Letting him make love to you?" Karen finished for her this time. "Just close?"

"To be honest, I almost begged *him* at one point." The thought still mortified her and she felt her face flush painfully.

Karen looked stunned. "You? The last of the dinosaurs?" she squeaked, then blinked twice as the rest of what Jillian had said sank in. "You mean he resisted?" Her dark curls bounced as she shook her head in disbelief. "That doesn't sound the least bit like our good friend Matt. In fact, the standing joke in college was that if you weren't that kind of girl, you didn't go out with Matt or you would be. It just sort of happened."

Jillian could believe it.

"I have to admit, though, Matt always dated girls who knew what was what," Karen added.

"You met him in college?" Jillian knew her fascination with the subject was about as healthy as a mouse's fascination with a cobra.

Karen nodded. "Jim grew up in the same area of Colorado as Matt, so shortly after I met Jim, I met Matt, too."

"Jim and Matt have been friends all their lives?"

"Not exactly. Until college they didn't associate much. Matt was several years ahead of Jim in school and I guess he was always a loner. I don't think he had much of a childhood."

Jillian sighed deeply and propped her chin in her hand. Knowing she wasn't the only one who thought he'd had an unhappy childhood didn't help much. She'd always been a real softie for anyone who hadn't grown up with lots of love and concern. Matt's tough-guys-are-self-sufficient attitude made her want to ensure that he didn't totally miss out on Grandma's kind of affection. "Yeah, I got the impression that Matt's childhood lacked a lot. He hinted that he grew up on the wrong side of the tracks, so to speak."

"Back then that was probably true," her friend agreed, "but most of the area around his place has been rebuilt in the past ten years. He's sitting on some prime real estate in the middle of several resort areas. He's worth a fortune. And you ought to see his house. It's beautiful. Since Jim's family has left the area, we borrow it when we go out to ski."

Jillian shook her head, grinning wryly. "You mean all my sympathy for poor practically homeless Matt has been wasted?"

"Well, he is homeless, to all intents and purposes." Karen laughed. "But it isn't because he doesn't have anywhere to go. He has homes all over the place. I know for sure he has apartments in Wichita and Kansas City. If you can call them that. Ugh.'' She shuddered. ''White walls, shades on the windows, the bare basics of furniture—you feel like you're walking into a rental company's showroom. When he's in Denver, he usually stays with his sister. Sometimes he lives out of motels for a month at a time. I've even known him to camp out in the office of one of his stores. He keeps clothes here, there and everywhere, and what he doesn't have with him, he buys when he needs it. It's really strange. Especially considering his house.''

''The one in Colorado?''

''Yeah. It's the house he grew up in. He bought it when he started making money and he totally rebuilt and modernized it. Then the old man who lived next to them died and left Matt his rickety old place and the five acres it sat on. That house simply *had* to come down—it was a real firetrap, so now Matt has lots of space around him. It's an isolated little hideaway right in the middle of Mecca.''

''And he doesn't spend much time there? Why not? Is it because of his stores?''

Karen rolled her eyes in an expression that clearly indicated Matt was crazy. ''Jim says the stores are so well organized Matt could check in once a year and never worry about them, but of course, that isn't his way. He seems to thrive on the traveling.''

''So my impression wasn't all that far off.''

''Not if you thought he was a drifter,'' Karen acknowledged, then qualified her remark. ''He'd be a real gypsy if he didn't have money. That's just the way he is. If it wasn't for his stores, he wouldn't know what to do with himself.''

Jillian relaxed against the back of her chair and filed away Karen's information for future reference. ''That explains why he can't decide whether or not to sell them.''

''You know about that?'' Karen's eyebrows rose a notch.

''He said he borrowed the cabin instead of going to his sister's for Christmas so he could think about it.''

Karen was looking suspicious again. ''Matt's usually very quiet about personal business. I thought he'd only discussed his plans with Jim and his lawyer.''

Jillian smiled, enjoying the thought that Matt had trusted her enough to discuss his ''personal business.''

''I think a lot of his indecision has to do with the old man,'' Karen went on. ''But of course, I get all my information secondhand through Jim. He says Matt wants to sell, but he doesn't think he will. Matt feels guilty, like he's turning his back on the chance the old man gave him, betraying his confidence. Did you get that impression?''

''He didn't tell me that much.'' Jillian faced the fact that any ''personal business'' Matt had shared with her had been merely to fill time. ''I think he thinks I'm an airhead. And I have to admit, I had mush for brains most of the time we were at the cabin together.''

''I can't imagine why,'' Karen teased. ''Which reminds me. Somehow, you got off the subject. What happened with Harrison? Did he just break the engagement without giving you a chance to explain? I tried to tell him about the mess Jim and I made of things when he called Christmas Eve, but he cut me off.''

"I explained. He was sympathetic until . . ."

"Yes?" Karen urged after a moment.

"Well, until I broke the engagement." Seeing Karen speechless for a third time in one day made Jillian laugh. "Close your mouth, Karen," she said, reaching across the table to chuck her friend under the chin.

"You were right. I was marrying him for all the wrong reasons." Jillian looked down at her hands and studied the intertwined fingers. "At first, he didn't take it very well. Then he decided I'd change my mind when I had time to think about how perfectly suited we were. He just left." She shrugged, realizing that their parting had been as innocuous as their relationship.

She'd hashed and rehashed the whole thing. Her engagement had been based on sheer terror at the thought of not having a soul in the world. Matt had pinpointed that fact almost immediately.

Poor Harrison. She probably owed him a better explanation than she'd given at the cabin, but things had sort of dissolved and that was that. "Now, *you* make sense of it all. What do you think?"

"You aren't going to like what I think."

"Since when did that stop you."

"I've told you from the beginning that I thought Harrison wasn't right for you, but . . ."

"And I've already admitted you were right."

"What's changed, Jilly? You'd still be engaged to Harrison if Matt hadn't been around."

"No. I just needed some time. I would have eventually come to my senses."

Karen pursed her lips and shook her head. "Then as far as you're concerned, the only thing that happened is that you realized you were marrying Harrison for the wrong reasons?"

"I guess that about covers it."

"So where does that leave Matt?"

Jillian got up to refill their coffee cups. "Where he's always been, I guess." She shrugged. "We really hit it off—don't jump to conclusions. I mean personally. I liked him and he liked me after we got over the initial shock. He let me talk about Grandma and cry on his shoulder. I didn't come home depressed like I was after Thanksgiving. It was nice." She sighed deeply. "Matt's intriguing, but any relationship I had with him would be as disastrous, if not more so, than the one I just got out of with Harrison."

"None for me," Karen said putting one hand over her cup as Jillian would have poured her more coffee. "I don't think you're right, but I suppose time will tell."

"I don't think time will have anything to do with it. I'll never see him again." Jillian gave another long sigh.

"Are you afraid to see him again?"

Jillian turned to put the pot back on its warmer. "Don't be silly," she scoffed, but had the squeamish feeling that she wasn't exactly getting stars for honesty. "What would be the point? He isn't interested in any permanent kind of relationship and I'm not interested in the kind of relationship he seems to want. I don't think either of us would be satisfied with being just friends. I'd probably end up as his lover, then be devastated when he left."

"Well, at least you didn't get yourself in over your head. That's something." Karen grabbed her purse off the corner of the table. "You're even close to figuring out why you were going to marry Harrison in the first place."

Jillian eyed her warily, curious but afraid she wouldn't like whatever Karen had to say. "I thought I'd already admitted that."

Karen shook her head. "No. You admitted you didn't want to be alone. But that's not the reason you agreed to marry Harrison."

"Oh?"

"You settled for him because you knew he couldn't hurt you. You didn't care enough to be hurt."

Jillian started to deny it but Karen stopped her. "Are you hurting now? Over anything that has to do with Harrison?' she added when Jillian would have nodded.

"So why do you think you'd be devastated if Matt left you?" Karen shrugged into her coat. "All those psychology classes I've had to take weren't wasted. I've used them to figure out how you managed to stay so untouched all this time."

Jillian frowned and sank down into her chair, pulling her feet up under her robe. She didn't bother telling Karen she really didn't want to hear her theories, because she knew it wouldn't do any good.

Karen took a deep breath. "How much do you remember about your parents?"

Jillian shrugged. "Not much."

"But when they died, you must have been crushed and confused. You were old enough to be hurt that someone you loved had left you, but not really old enough to understand that they had no choice."

"I don't know. I can't remember." Jillian wrapped her arms around her knees defensively.

"And your first love?"

"Jeremy?" Remembering the dimple-cheeked, dark-haired little boy always made her smile.

Karen nodded. "You fell in love with him in second grade."

"Yeah, he'd pull my curls and drive me crazy."

"Until his folks moved to Wichita when you were fifteen," Karen said meaningfully.

"If he hadn't moved, I'd probably still be moping around over him. And the feelings were only mutual some of the time. When he turned a little bit of attention my way, I walked around in a daze for months."

"You said you cried yourself to sleep every night for six months after he left."

"I was fifteen years old, for Pete's sake! *Everything* was high drama at the time."

The smile in Karen's eyes was warm. "I know. I was the same way, but—"

"It was the best thing that could have happened, Karen. After he moved, I cut out the hero worship and started dating around. I started having a lot of fun."

Jillian's cramped position had grown uncomfortable. She stood up, feeling restless.

"But did it convince you to play it a little too safe?" Karen asked. "You can't get hurt if you don't care too much." She headed for the front door.

Jillian followed her. "I think you're right. You've been taking your education far too seriously," she said lightly. "And how come I care so much about you?"

"I'm harmless." Karen said, smiling. "And all those guys you dated were harmless, too. That's the only reason you've gotten this old without winding up in someone's bed."

"And all that stuff Grandma taught me had nothing to do with it?" Jillian said wryly.

"Maybe partially."

They looked at each other for a silent moment. "Harrison was safe," Karen reiterated, as if she couldn't leave things on an easy note. "But Matt's a different story, huh? *He* could leave a few scars. Are you sure you didn't fall in love with him?"

Before Jillian could answer, Karen rushed on. "Is that why you ran back here like a scared rabbit?"

"My reason for being there ceased to exist."

"But you didn't have any reason to hurry back either, did you? Matt told me he asked you to stay. What are you going to do here for the rest of Christmas vacation? Stay in your apartment and be depressed?"

Jillian had an answer for that one. "I'm going to go through the rest of Grandma's things and start the new year with a clean slate. And in January, I'm going to check into using some of Grandma's insurance money to go back to school."

Karen hugged her impulsively. "I'm delighted, Jilly. I've always loved you the way you are, but I won't worry about you quite so much when you join the real world and quit playing..." She searched for a word.

"June Cleaver?" Jillian offered automatically.

"Exactly. Stop watching reruns. We've come a long way from that." She tucked her scarf into her coat. "I've got to go. I'll give Matt your phone number. He asked for it earlier—"

"Don't you dare!"

"Jillian." Karen threw up her hands, exasperated. "I'm not going to play go-between. I left that behind in junior high. It's not as though I said I was going to give it to a total stranger."

"I told him I didn't want to see him again. I meant it. It's a dead end. Besides, I doubt the question will even come up. He's probably already written me off as one of those ships passing in the night. That's all it was and you're making a whole lot out of nothing. We just happened to get snowed in at your cabin at the same time."

"Well, Jilly, it's your life, but if I were you... Never mind. But please, please, think about what I've said." She hugged her again. "I'm glad you're back in almost one piece."

"I'll give you a call later in the week." Karen stepped outside. "If Matt *does* happen to ask, I'll let him know you aren't interested," she added, closing the door behind her.

Jillian had the strong urge to fling it open and argue with her, but she wasn't sure what she would argue about.

CHAPTER EIGHT

By FOUR O'CLOCK New Year's Eve, Jillian was loading the last of the superfluous contents of her spare bedroom into the trunk of her little car. She'd spent the days since she'd returned going through Grandma's things and sorting out her emotional closets.

Well, most of them. Karen's unfortunate attempt at playing psychologist stuck in her mind like a needle on one of Grandma's worn-out records. Okay, so Karen could be right about her reason for having chosen Harrison. But knowing that didn't change anything with Matt.

If Karen was right, Jillian knew she'd better stop dwelling on Matt, but he'd entrenched himself in her thoughts as though he belonged there. Why would her heart choose someone guaranteed to make her re-learn the same old lesson? Somehow, she had to relegate him to her mental file labeled ''fond memories.'' That was where he belonged.

She lifted the last cache of odds and ends off the floor as the doorbell rang.

The door was ajar from her last trip to the car. ''Come on in Karen,'' she hollered. ''I'm in the spare bedroom. I'll be out in a minute.''

''And no,'' she added under her breath, ''I'm not going out with your friend tonight.''

Although Karen had been trying to convince Jillian that her only motive was a pair of wasted reservations, she suspected this was part of Karen's game plan to heal Jillian's "broken" heart.

Kicking the bedroom door open with her foot, she leaned the heavy box against the doorjamb, got a better grip on it, then pushed aside the tangle of hair covering her eyes.

"I wouldn't recommend leaving the front door unlocked. Anyone could walk in," a familiar voice said from the end of the short hall.

Jillian's head jerked up and the box angled precariously. Matt was immediately beside her, lifting the load out of her arms.

"Hi, Jake," he said, smiling at her dumbstruck look.

"How did you get here?" Jillian found her voice, then ran to catch up with him as he strode up the hall with her burden.

"Where do you want this?" he asked, ignoring her question.

"What are you doing here?"

"Carrying a box, I think. Where do you want it?" he repeated.

"The car," she answered automatically. She opened the front door for him and led him down the stairs, pointing out icy spots as they made their way to the parking lot.

After he stashed the box inside, Jillian slammed the trunk closed. She suddenly wished she didn't look as if she'd taken a dust shower, and she brushed a cloud of it off her jeans. She couldn't help beaming; her smile felt as bright as the sunshine. "You're still taking over, I see."

"Yeah." He grinned, thumbing a streak of dirt from her cheek. Then he took her arm and guided her up the stairs. "From the looks of things, someone needs to."

"Why?"

"Because I hate to think how you're going to end up if you insist on leaving your apartment door unlocked and wandering outside in December without a coat. Your guardian angel must be slipping."

"Next you'll be saying she sent you."

"Nope. Totally my own idea." He shut the apartment door behind them and removed his coat, pitching it onto the rocking chair.

"You may as well put that back on," Jillian said.

He ignored her as he wandered from one end of the main room to the other, checking the layout of her apartment.

"I suppose I have Karen to thank for this."

"Jim, actually." He stopped in front of her, the left side of his mouth twitching upward. "You *look* happy to see me, even if you don't sound that way."

"I am." Heaven help her, she was, and it made her feel claustrophobic. She inched away from him and the urge to touch him. Having him here was probably far more dangerous than leaving her front door unlocked twenty-four hours a day.

Jillian lit on the first thing that came into her mind. "I thought you were staying at the cabin until after New Year's." It seemed like forever since she'd been there.

"I planned to. It was too quiet after you left."

Her smile grew wider and she willed it to fade—to no avail. "I thought you wanted peace and quiet so you could make a decision about selling your stores."

"I've decided."

"Oh?"

"I'm selling. I've been with Jim most of the day. He has a lot of paperwork to complete before I can move ahead with the deal." He took a step that brought him closer. "That's why I'm here. I want you to help me celebrate this evening."

Jillian frowned. "I see you took me seriously when I said I'd rather not see you again."

"You have plans?"

"No, but—"

"Good."

"But it doesn't make any difference since you're leaving," she finished.

"You made up with Harry?"

What did Harrison have to do with it? She wondered if Matt's accident had impaired his hearing. The wicked red scar he tried to hide by parting his hair differently certainly hadn't impaired his looks. He still made her blood rush and her knees shake.

"Would he be upset that I'm here?" Matt clarified.

She was tempted to lie, but couldn't. "I haven't even caught a glimpse of Harrison." Her chin tilted up determinedly. "I hadn't planned to brave the mobs tonight, though. I want to spend a quiet evening at home."

"Sounds good to me. I'll bring the—"

"Alone." She picked up his coat and handed it to him, careful not to touch him.

"Why?" Matt put on his coat.

She stuttered and stammered, hunting for a reason, then looked at him, dead-on. "You can't ask why."

Matt shrugged again, seemingly at a loss for words, then turned and walked toward the door. "See you, Jillian."

As the door closed behind him, the apartment closed in around her. Jillian took a deep breath and decided she'd better call and accept Karen's "wasted reservations" after all—with or without the "date." It was either that or spend New Year's Eve wishing she'd taken Matt up on his invitation.

"Not a good way to start the new year," she mumbled, catching a glimpse of herself in the mirror hanging over the small desk. A dirty-faced urchin stared back at her. The navy kerchief hadn't managed to control her hair, and pale blond wisps drifted every which way. Dusty smudges decorated her face, accenting her rosy-tinged skin. Her eyes looked too wide, too bright.

The flush she attributed to overexertion, but the dazed look in her eyes could only be blamed on Matt.

The fact that he'd bothered to find her meant nothing, she assured her reflection. They'd shared a very pleasant Christmas, despite all the problems. And adversity usually caused people to feel close. Why wouldn't he want to keep in touch?

The word *touch* made her shiver and she ran through the whole litany of reasons for not seeing him again as she hurried to the kitchen to call Karen.

Her line was busy.

"I'll take my bath," she decided aloud, "then try her again."

She was sitting in hot water with bubbles almost to her chin when she heard the front door open.

Dammit! Hadn't she locked the door after Matt left? She quickly glanced around the small room, aware that she didn't even have a robe with her, much less a rolling pin or a lead pipe.

Her best bet seemed to be to sit tight and wait out the intruder. Maybe it was the expected visit from Karen. She pulled at a towel and it slithered off the rod, and she stood up in the water as she wrapped it around herself and quietly reached to turn the lock on the bathroom door.

"Jillian?"

Matt's voice, mere inches away on the other side of the door, caught her off guard and she slipped. Her hands flailed, her body went flying.

Water splashed everywhere, along with most of the scented bubbles, and she landed with a soft thud in the bottom of the tub.

"Are you all right?" The handle turned and Matt's head peered around the edge of the door. His eyes narrowed with concern.

"No, Matt, I'm not all right," she answered when she'd finally caught her breath. "Get out. You almost killed me." He had the decency to look guilty as his head disappeared and he yanked the door shut. "What are you doing here again?"

"I brought wine and steaks for our celebration."

"Oh, Matt," she wailed, irritated. Exasperated. "Can't you take a hint? I told you I was going to spend the evening by myself."

"Come out and let's talk about it."

Jillian rose, gingerly checking her body for broken bones, and stepped out of the tub. Her towel, which had taken the dive with her, was drenched and dripping on the floor. "Hand me my robe. It's on the hook on the back of my bedroom door," she ordered, knowing that Matt would stand outside the bathroom until she gave in. "And a dry towel while you're at it. They're in the closet next to the bedroom."

When she heard him return, she stuck out her bare arm to foil any plan he might have about bringing the requested items in. She emerged after only a few minutes and faced him, aware that her dripping hair and faded chenille robe lent her the appearance of a scruffy drowned rat. Too bad; she hadn't invited him here to see.

"Most people wait to be invited before they come barging into someone's home." She crossed her arms defensively.

"Would you have invited me in?"

She wished he'd quit with the ear-to-ear grin. She couldn't think.

"I thought not. I was glad that you didn't lock the door this time either, but I hope you don't make a practice of it. Now. How are we going to celebrate?"

"I told you. I'm going to stay home tonight. Alone," she added as he started to agree. "Considering the past year, I feel I need some time by myself this New Year's Eve. You understand?"

He nodded. "I just don't happen to think you're right." His voice lowered. "We can fix steaks here—" he motioned to a brown paper sack he'd set next to the bathroom door "—or we can go out with Karen and

Jim. She assures me they have extra reservations. Which will it be?''

She must have looked as surprised as she felt, because he laughed. He had a wonderful laugh. ''See? I've given you a choice.'' Matt stepped nearer, until only a wisp of air separated them. ''You wouldn't want me to celebrate alone, would you?'' He smiled, gently stroking the side of her neck, then following the line of her collarbone with his thumb.

She tried to move away, but her heel met the wall and she was trapped. ''There isn't any point in going on with this, Matt. You—we—I don't want to—''

''I know,'' he hushed her. ''But I needed to see you again. Away from the cabin. That wasn't real.''

Too weak to argue, Jillian sighed and nodded, then said breathlessly, ''But let's go out with Jim and Karen. I don't think hanging around here would be much of a celebration.'' She shrugged his hands away and willed herself to concentrate on getting ready. ''I guess I'd better finish my bath,'' she hinted.

He glanced at his watch. ''The reservations are for eight. I'll pick you up in a hour.''

''We surely don't need to leave that early.''

''How dress-up is this, anyway?''

''It's probably one of the dressier New Year's Eve parties in town.''

Matt's eyes rested on the sagging V of her robe and she tugged the flaps closed. She realized she'd made matters worse when she heard his sharp intake of breath. The worn chenille clung to her damp body and prominently displayed her breasts.

Matt exhaled long and audibly, and looked down at her bare feet. ''We need to leave soon because I'll have to go by the mall and pick up something to wear. While we're there I should stop in at the store and talk to Molly."

"If it's going to be a—"

"It's not a problem if I can use your phone," he replied, lacing his thumbs into his belt loops. "What are you wearing? We could buy you something new while we're at it."

"I'll wear my black taffeta," she decided quickly.

"If you insist. An hour then?"

She nodded silently and was in the bathroom running the water before she realized she'd acquiesced to everything he'd suggested except new clothes. She hadn't even waited until he was out of the apartment to escape back into the bathroom. As far as she knew, he was still in the kitchen using the phone. She double-checked the lock on the door.

She shouldn't have agreed to go out with him! As long as he didn't intrude on her day-to-day world she should eventually be able to pigeonhole him with other pleasant memories. He'd said the time at the cabin was unreal for him, too.

She climbed out of the tepid water and finished the rest of her preparations absentmindedly.

Maybe she should have chosen to stay here. Karen was going to analyze everything either of them said or did, and Jillian would hear about it, in detail, for the next ten years.

And it would take Karen three seconds or less to know Jillian was in love with Matt.

Suddenly, Jillian's hand shook so much that she had to put down her mascara.

She *was* in love with him.

Her fist pressed heavily against her chest, trying to quell the relieved yet terrified throbbing. She was relieved that she'd finally admitted the truth to herself, but the admission wasn't worth a thing. Investing every last cent she owned in swampland in Florida would have made more sense. And probably have given her a better return on her investment.

But what if— She cautioned herself not to get her hopes up.

She did anyway. He *might* love her. She knew he cared. He'd never said he didn't want to fall in love— just that he wouldn't get married.

She shook her head, then stood back and admired herself in the mirror.

Picking up the lovely necklace Matt had given her, she fastened the slender chain about her neck. It shimmered against her bare skin and, combined with her bemused glow, provided a finishing touch. The bells tinkled softly.

Ring out the old year, ring in the new. Suddenly the new year brimmed with possibilities. She closed her eyes and prayed for her wildest dreams.

THE WIDE HEM of Jillian's short black dress rustled against the leg of Matt's jeans as he pulled her gently through the doors leading into the quiet mall. They went into one store after another. In one, he picked up an expensive electric razor and a small bottle of aftershave. In the next he bought dress shoes. He couldn't seem to keep his eyes off her as he led her toward the one men's store that carried formal wear.

"It'll be a little while, Mr. Carson," the clerk said, looking at her watch.

"By seven?"

She looked skeptical. "Mrs. Maxwell is coming in to do the alterations, but she isn't here yet."

"I'm sure she'll make it. Do you have big plans for the night?"

"My roommate and I are having a hell of a party." The young woman grinned. "We'll probably start the new year looking for a new apartment."

"Sounds like fun."

Jillian grudgingly admired Matt's manner. The girl was smiling in spite of the fact that she was going to be late to her own party. Of course, it didn't hurt that he handed her a fifty-dollar bill for her "inconvenience," then added a matching one for the absent Mrs. Maxwell.

He piled the other things he would need beside the cash register and signed his name to the account slip. Then with a large sack slung over his shoulder, he cupped Jillian's elbow in his other hand and guided her out of the store.

"I want to buy you something new." Matt turned to her. His gaze slid the length of her body, easing past the bolero-style lamb's wool jacket to the draped fabric snugly outlining her figure. He skimmed the short full skirt and then took his time admiring her shapely legs. Her dainty high-heels brought them almost eye to eye, and that was where his look rested when the inspection was over. "But I can't see any room for improvement."

She glowed as he led her toward Carson's.

"Matt?" An immaculately groomed, white-haired saleswoman greeted him. "I didn't expect you until the end of next week."

"Hi, Molly." He grinned, tugging Jillian out in front of him. "Molly manages this store for me," he explained as he introduced them.

Molly smiled warmly. "I need to pass on a few messages, Matt, then as things are pretty slow, I thought I'd close a little early. I'm watching my granddaughters this evening."

"You go ahead," he said. "Jillian and I will close while we're waiting for my tux."

He and Molly began discussing business, and Jillian studied the store. The plush mauve carpeting blended beautifully with gray, pink and mauve painted walls. Chrome and glass counters held breathtaking jewelry. One corner of the large room was secluded by a padded room divider upholstered in silver brocade.

No one would have guessed in a million years that the man standing over there in the lumberjack costume was the one behind this soft, romantic atmosphere.

She turned to the glass case in the middle of the store, absently staring at the engagement rings and wedding sets.

What ordinary man wouldn't trade his ordinary job, wife and 2.2 children for Matt's life-style? Matt went where he wanted, spent what he wanted. He owned seven successful stores, which, if Molly was anything to go by, were managed by warm, efficient people. He traveled.

She suddenly didn't want to see this part of Matt's life. It was too perfect. Of course he'd never be interested in any of the make-believe games she'd played earlier tonight.

"I want to show you something," Matt said quietly, resting his hand on her shoulder. He steered her clear of the rings and into the business end of the store. "Did you find it, Molly?" he asked as they entered the office.

The elegant older woman handed him a small wooden box. "I'll be off now."

Matt locked the back door behind her, then sat Jillian in a chair by a large industrial-looking desk.

He propped himself on one corner, half-sitting as he opened the box and held it out to her. "Thought you might like to see some of John's handiwork," he said, proud as a boy just learning to whistle.

The perfectly matched pair of butterflies rested against the yellowed satin lining of the box. Their exquisite silver filigreed wings caught the light and seemed to quiver in readiness to fly. The tiny bodies were inlaid with a sliver of dark polished stone. She thought it might be onyx. "They're beautiful, Matt," she whispered. "He made these by hand?" She glanced up. From Matt's pleased expression, she guessed she'd shown she was appropriately impressed.

She looked back down at the box. "And this is one of the boxes you made?" she wondered aloud, turning it over.

"Yeah," he replied, almost shyly.

She ran her fingers across the smooth top, picturing boyish hands, a bent head, intense concentration. She ached for the child who had so hungrily accepted tender nurturing from an outwardly rough but inwardly gentle old man.

Swiftly blinking away a spot of moisture from the corner of her eye, she handed back the box. He pocketed it. "I would love to have met John."

"You'd have liked him," Matt assured her in a rough voice. "I suppose I should go man the front. It's still a quarter of an hour till closing time. I probably should keep the store open since we have to wait anyway. You can stay here if you like."

"I may as well join you."

"No one will be in in the short time we have left," he promised, reentering the showroom.

A young couple rushed in, as if to prove him wrong, and hurried over to the rings in the center of the store. "Can I help you? I do work here," Matt assured the startled pair.

The man hesitated. "I hope we aren't too late to look at your engagement rings?" The woman smiled and tightened her grip on his hand. "Janet has just agreed to marry me and I want to make it official before she changes her mind."

That's how it's supposed to be, thought Jillian, as Matt excused himself with a discreet nod and led the couple to the partition at the back. There had been none of the excitement, none of the joy so blatantly displayed on this couple's faces in her arrangement with Harrison.

Matt made her feel both those things.

The clerk from the men's store breezed in carrying Matt's tux over her shoulder. "We didn't quite make it," she puffed. "I hope that doesn't spoil your plans for the evening."

Jillian gestured to the feet showing beneath the bottom of the partition. "It's just as well. Matt's busy."

"That's the way it usually goes." She rolled her eyes as she handed Jillian the suit bag. "I've got to run, but you two have a nice time tonight."

"You, too," Jillian called, but the other woman was gone before the words were out.

The mall was dim and barren now, filled with a tomblike silence. Carson's was the one oasis of brightness.

Jillian decided Matt wouldn't mind if she pulled the heavy glass doors shut across the side entrance.

That done, she picked up the suit, took it to the office and sat down to wait, immediately slipping into a daydream.

"I'm sorry, Jake," Matt said sometime later, his voice making her jump guiltily at the thoughts she'd been having. "I didn't mean to take so long."

"That's okay." Jillian set her feet back on the floor, smoothing the folds of her dress self-consciously. She wasn't dressed for propping her feet up on desks any more than he was dressed for selling engagement rings. "Did you make a sale?"

"Yep," he said, "poor jerk." When she started to rise to the bait, he winked at her, then grabbed the tuxedo off the door. "I'll be ready in no time."

CHAPTER NINE

SOON, MATT WAS turning off lights, helping her into her jacket and ushering her out the back of the store to his Blazer.

"You realize we've missed our meal," he said, reversing wildly out of the parking space and tearing across the empty lot.

"I realized it was getting late," she agreed cheerfully. It seemed as if nothing could deflate her ballooning high. Even Matt's calling that happy man who'd bought the engagement ring a "jerk" hadn't put a pinhole in it.

"I don't know about you, but I'm starving."

Jillian's stomach rumbled in response and Matt whipped into one of the parking lots along fast-food alley.

Recovering from her initial surprise, she joined him on the pavement.

"I'm sorry." He caught her hand and swung her around to face him. The light filtering down from the street lamp lent his eyes an extra intensity. "This isn't what I had in mind, but I don't think we'll get in anywhere else tonight without a long wait. Besides, I have a thing about junk food."

"Me, too," she said, barely keeping her voice from trembling. The one thing she couldn't take from Matt was intensity. It turned her body into jelly and her brain into sawdust. She escaped toward the bright entrance. "Are you going to feed me?"

Still in a daze, Jillian merely said "same thing" when it came her turn to order. Matt's brow lifted in surprise. "With lots of ketchup," she added. She hadn't the faintest idea what she was getting, but ketchup seemed like a safe bet. She went to find them a booth.

While Matt waited for their food, she and the young man at the counter examined Matt's tux.

He looked devastating in it. She'd expected him to be stiff and uncomfortable, but he wore the suit as casually as he wore his flannel shirts and jeans. The black fabric emphasized shoulders broad enough to lean on. The white shirt contrasted with his slightly weathered complexion and perfectly matched his teeth when he smiled. She'd always thought dress clothes were designed for tall, elegantly slender men, but they made Matt's more powerful physique look fluid and graceful as he moved toward her now, carrying the tray in one hand.

"Your dinner, *madame*." He smiled, sliding onto the bench across from her.

"Didn't your attire meet with his approval?" she asked conversationally, frowning at the two enormous hamburgers he'd placed in front of her.

"He thought it might be nice for the prom if it came in canary yellow." Matt piled ketchup packets beside her large order of fries. "I can't quite picture it myself."

Jillian looked up at him. "I can see why he likes it. You look great, Matt." She meant the remark as a careless compliment. It sounded like heartfelt hero worship.

"You've got to stop looking at me like that, Jillian. I don't mind telling you that you're sending my thoughts in directions I didn't mean them to go."

She felt a flush spread. She'd taken off her jacket and even the skin above the stand-up front of her dress felt stained with pink.

Jillian fought a tingly shiver and looked away from him. "Have you thought any more about what you're going to do when your deal goes through?" she asked. "Maybe you should go into some kind of marketing. You must like selling things—at least you seemed to enjoy it tonight."

Matt bit into his sandwich. "I don't enjoy selling per se," he admitted. "And I'm out of practice. I don't get to do much of it anymore." He shrugged. "I liked selling John's earrings door to door, though. I made a lot of people happy. It was satisfying.

"Which reminds me." Matt shifted and reached into the inside pocket of his jacket. "Here." He pulled out the small wooden box he'd made. "I want you to have these."

"John's earrings?" She jerked her hand away.

"We're not going to go through this again, are we?" Taking hold of her hand, he placed the box on her palm. Her fingers curled up protectively. "No strings," he said, cupping her hand between his.

"I didn't think that," she said. "But I can't take these. You probably don't have many more of them and what you've got you'd better keep."

His hands tightened around hers. "This is the last pair, actually. I've held on to them for years."

The air in the bright and silent fast-food restaurant became electric. The one customer who'd shared their solitude was gone, and even the boy behind the counter had deserted them.

"Matt," she said hesitantly, "wouldn't you like to save them for someone very special?"

"I did." Neither of them spoke for long moments, then he released her and picked up a French fry. "My mother and my sister both have several pairs." She had to strain to hear his low voice above the quiet background music. "I used to give them quite regularly to other friends."

She didn't need to ask what kind of other friends he spoke of.

"They aren't ever going to do me any good. I want you to have this last pair." He finally looked up at her again. "John would have liked you. I think he would have liked knowing they're in your keeping."

The lump in Jillian's throat refused to dissolve and her vision became by blurred with tears. "Look what you're doing, Matt," she whispered hoarsely. "All that time I spent on my makeup, and you're going to have it smeared all over my face." She dabbed at the corner of her eye with a knuckle. "You don't know how much this means to me. I'll take them and treasure them," she added quietly, "but on one condition."

He looked at her quizzically.

"If you ever change your mind, if you should find someone you wished you'd saved them for—"

"Back to the inevitable marriage discussion, huh?" He regarded her with open amusement, suddenly reverting to his old self.

"You never know." Jillian lifted one bare shoulder defensively. "Things change."

"Yes, they do." His mouth curved into a smile that forced her to smile at him in return.

She looked at him soberly. "I mean it, Matt. If they do change, I would never feel you were out of line if you wanted them back. We'll consider it—" she searched for the right word "—joint custody."

He threw back his head and laughed outright. She couldn't help but regret her choice of terms. "You never quit, do you, Jake?" His tone was rich with enjoyment. "Does this mean I have permanent visitation rights?" Underlying the teasing note was a serious one.

Her heart swelled until it seemed to fill her chest. How could she ever turn him away? "I guess," she agreed softly and they were back to a tense and dangerously charged silence.

"You'd better eat," Matt said finally. "We're going to miss the dancing and champagne if we don't get a move on."

"Can I keep these in your pocket for now?" She handed the little box back to him. "I didn't bring a purse."

"I'd assumed that's what the front of your dress was for." He grinned, gazing at the ruffled bodice of her strapless dress.

She blushed and directed her attention to the huge meal she'd unknowingly ordered. She wasn't the least bit hungry.

"So-o-o?" Silence between them was too provocative. "What are you going to do after you sell your stores? Have you had time to think about it yet?"

"I toyed with a concept years ago. Maybe now is the right time for it."

"What is it?"

"When I first thought about this, I wanted to do it in conjunction with the stores, but I realized that wouldn't do either my old business or this new idea justice. Have you ever been to Branson, Missouri?"

"Silver Dollar City? Grandma and I went there twice and it was fascinating."

"Silver Dollar City reminds me of John—watching the craftsmen work, hearing them explain why things are done a certain way. I'd like to try something similar in Colorado. A colony of sorts for craftsmen."

"And women," Jillian inserted.

"And craftswomen." Matt chuckled. "No rides or shows, but something that would give people a look at how beautiful things used to be made."

"That sounds like a wonderful idea." It genuinely did. And it would help ease any lingering guilt he might have about turning his back on the start John had given him. Her eyes were on Matt as she idly picked up a French fry, not realizing that it was dripping ketchup until she felt wetness against her skin.

She reached for her napkin, self-consciously glancing at Matt to see if he'd noticed.

He'd noticed. His hand was frozen in midair, his own French fry hovering as he strained to see over the ruffles.

Jillian's mouth went dry. Matt's eyes jolted up to meet hers. He swallowed hard, then blinked as if trying to erase the longing apparent in them.

"See I told you the front of that dress was good for something besides piquing curiosity," he said roughly, adding "I've never been jealous of ketchup before."

She blotted it up quickly.

"You're making me regret all the promises I made to myself tonight." He picked up the napkin she'd just put down and flattened it between his hands, gently smoothing out the wrinkles.

Her skin quivered as if he'd touched her. To disguise her reaction, she laughed nervously. She had to say something. "You are rude, crude and lewd, Matthew Carson. I'll never be able to wear this dress again without thinking..."

His eyes reflected his pleasure at that idea.

"I don't know why I like you." Her words came out low and shaky.

"I know why."

"Why?" Jillian wondered if she'd ever be able to breathe normally again.

"Because it's hard not to like someone who likes you as much as I do," he answered simply. "Despite the fact that I'm rude, crude and..."

"And lewd," Jillian supplied.

"Yeah. Now let's go off and join Karen and Jim, before I can't remember what we wanted to celebrate."

THEY DROVE to the big hotel where the New Year's Eve bash was taking place. Matt parked his vehicle and they made it halfway to the entrance.

As he guided her across the snow-crusted parking lot, his arm slipped around her, and suddenly her chest was hard against his. "I can't do this any longer." He sighed heavily. "I promised myself we'd keep it friendly but I've been dying to kiss you all day."

He followed the words with the action. And then, she was on tiptoe, responding as if she'd never get enough of him. He didn't stop until his hands slipped beneath her coat to stroke the soft skin of her back.

"The bad thing, Jake," he murmured against her lips, "is that I still want you." He raised his head, savoring her with his eyes.

Jillian let her heart open wide. *I love him. He makes me crazy with wanting. He can hurt me like I've never been hurt before—and I still want him.*

"I thought seeing you again under normal circumstances would make a difference. It has," he muttered thickly. "For the worse."

His hand tightened, pressing her even closer, his warmth enveloping her, protecting her from the cold night air. It felt like love.

He ran his fingers along the low back of her dress, and an ache grew deep inside her.

Whether he admits it or not, he loves me. She'd felt it since he'd walked into her apartment that afternoon. The feeling was even stronger now.

"I shouldn't have said anything." He started to turn away.

"No," she protested, "no, I'm..." She let the words drift away and stared up at him.

If she didn't take whatever he was willing to give, would she regret it? Yes, the answer came swift and sure. And if she *did* accept what he could give, would she regret it? Probably, she answered just as truthfully.

She'd begged him to make love to her at the cabin. Then, she wasn't sorry he hadn't. But now—now that she knew she loved him, now that she wasn't tied to Harrison—she didn't want her regrets to be based on not knowing what could have been.

She took a deep breath. He was the man she'd waited for all this time. She knew it as surely as she knew Grandma was smiling from her heaven.

Matt was studying her anxiously.

"The bad thing, Matt," she whispered slowly, "is that I want you, too."

Matt's brows rose as if he were afraid he'd misunderstood. "Are you saying...?"

"Yes."

His grin spread slowly. "Let's get out of here."

Matt didn't speak until they were almost back at her apartment. His arm tightened around her shoulders and he pulled her closer. "You're sure?"

"Yes."

He drew her out his door when he parked the car, as if reluctant to let go of her for even a minute.

She fumbled clumsily with the keys as they climbed the stairs. He took them from her impatiently and unlocked the door.

She turned to hang their coats in the closet, suddenly shy and reluctant to face him again.

"Come here," he growled, taking their coats and flinging them over the back of the nearest chair. He circled her with his arms. "Seven days is a long time to wait to unwrap a Christmas present."

Matt's kiss, his touch, made her tremble. Her fingers felt the heavy thud of his heart as they splayed against his chest. She relaxed in his arms enjoying the feeling of delicious weakness.

His lips covered hers, desperately at first, then with infinite tenderness. She moaned and he scattered warm kisses along the column of her throat, molding her to him with a wide sweeping stroke of his hand along her back. The sensation made her dizzy and her neck arched, giving him full access to the sensitive spot behind her ear. He covered the line of her jaw with his kisses until her breathing grew uneven.

Releasing her zipper, he smoothed her dress down her body, leaning back to feast with his eyes, exciting her with his obvious pleasure. She felt enchanted. Beautiful. He boldly examined the length of her, seeding confidence amid the uncertainty. "Jillian. I've never wanted anyone like I want you." Hunger throbbed in his voice.

"I've never felt this way before," she said, awed.

"I aim to please," Matt said, with the suggestion of a laugh. And the tuxedo jacket they'd spent so long waiting for landed in a heap on the end of the sofa, along with his tie.

She watched as his fingers released the tiny buttons of his stark white shirt, then he drew her to him again. His skin burned hers as he pressed her closer.

He braced her hips against his as he bent to shower kisses on her satiny skin.

When her legs grew too shaky to support her, he picked her up and carried her down the dark hall to her bedroom. His lips still on hers, he placed her gently on the bed, leaning on his elbows to keep his full weight from crushing her.

Jillian's hands ceased their restless wandering and settled on the muscular breadth of his shoulders. Her hips instinctively pressed against his. His murmur of satisfaction settled on her lips as he kissed her. Slowly, he explored her breasts while he unclasped her bra. Easing it away, his mouth lowered to taste her. "You're even more wonderful than I'd imagined."

Jillian moaned, wanting the wild sensations to go on, yet sure she'd die if they didn't end soon.

"Touch me, Jillian," he breathed impatiently, guiding her hand to the waistband of his slacks.

One finger stroked the velvety skin bared by his open shirt. He drew slightly away, enjoying her caress. Her hand shook nervously as it flattened against his chest.

"You're as shy as a virgin," he whispered, as if the idea amused and pleased him. Then his eyes jolted open.

Jillian's hand curled against his warm skin and his body tensed under her touch.

His eyes narrowed. "You are, aren't you?"

She nodded slowly, meeting his eyes even though she wanted to look away.

"Why didn't you tell me?" he asked hoarsely. He gently withdrew from her.

She tried to move closer. "Please, Matt," she finally managed to say. "Does it matter?"

"Why didn't you tell me?" he repeated. His jaw tightened spasmodically.

"I didn't think it was important," she said, reining in a growing uneasiness. "I thought you knew." She sat up and pulled the edge of the bedspread around her. "Besides, no one can stay a virgin forever." She'd expected him to appreciate the gift she'd saved for a lifetime.

Matt bolted from the bed and paced to the window, jamming his hands into the pockets of his dress pants so violently she expected the fabric to shred.

"Should *I* have asked if there were any strings attached?"

It was suddenly very cold in the room. Jillian got stiffly out of bed and walked to the closet. Away from him. Matt remained silent while she slipped into the heaviest, warmest, fleeciest robe she owned.

When she turned he was looking through her as if she weren't there.

"I finally understand how my father fell into the trap he did," he stated flatly.

"How?"

"The obligation he felt to my mother."

Jillian threw up her hands in exasperation. "What makes you think I want anything from you?"

His eyes focused. "Don't you?"

"No," she lied, and felt her heart tear and start to bleed. "You've forgotten that *I* made this choice. No one thinks anything of sleeping with anyone they want to. Why should I? I'm all grown-up now."

She watched as his doubt reared its ugly head. "Why me?" he demanded skeptically, taking a long stride toward her.

"It's a terrible job," she muttered sarcastically, "but someone has to do it."

"Damn it, Jillian—"

"Why shouldn't I choose you to take my virginity? You were willing. If you aren't now, why don't you just leave? I don't see any chains holding you here. No strings. See?" She raised her hands, spreading them to show there was nothing attached. "I knew what to expect. You warned me at the cabin. Remember?"

"But I didn't know.... I assumed Harrison..." He stopped and raked a weary hand through his thick hair.

"He didn't." Jillian's knees felt weak. She slumped down onto the bed. "Please, just go, Matt." She didn't want him to see her cry, and if he didn't get out of there soon, he was going to.

"I guess I should be glad I found out in time."

Jillian looked at him blankly.

"It could have been after it was too late, when the wronged virgin showed up pregnant. I'd be expected to 'do the right thing.' Isn't that how it works? It has for centuries."

For the first time in their brief acquaintance Jillian hated Matthew Carson, hated him as passionately as she loved him. "You surely weren't planning to go through with this without protection?" she asked angrily.

"You probably would have told me you were on the pill and I didn't need to worry about it."

Jillian's face turned a pasty, sickly pale and Matt groaned.

"I'm sorry. I shouldn't have said that." He stared blindly down at his hands. "I know you wouldn't do that."

He didn't move even when Jillian came closer. He stared at her, his own brand of self-torture reflected in his face.

"I don't understand any of this," she whispered. "You said that two consenting adults don't have to say

'I love you' to make love. I accepted that. I haven't asked for a human sacrifice. What did I do wrong?''

He groaned again and buried his head in his hands. "You're giving and warm, more than I dreamed anyone could be," he said softly.

"Then what—?"

He touched her for the first time since he'd left the bed, gripping her shoulders between his palms. "I'm not a giver, I'm a taker. But for all my selfish ways, I do feel guilt."

"That's your own fault."

"Do you think I want to feel this way?" Matt let his hands wander idly up and down her arms, as if he needed the contact. "Why do you think I've always limited my extracurricular activities to women who're playing the same game I am? No expectations. No excess emotion. Just pure and simple selfishness. You scratch my back, I'll scratch yours." He dropped his hands as if she was burning him. "That's not what was about to happen here. You don't fit the category, Jake. I feel responsible for you and you deserve more than I can give."

"Shouldn't that—"

He interrupted, berating himself. "With Harrison out of the picture there was nothing to stop me from having you. I convinced myself you were playing the same game because I wanted to believe it."

He threaded his fingers through the ends of her tumbled hair, watching the movement, avoiding her eyes.

Surely there was something she could do. Something she could say. She loved him. Anything was worth a try. "I can play your game," she offered.

He groaned as if she'd wounded him. Her fingers itched to erase the sad lines from his face, to turn the pain in his eyes back into delight.

"I don't want you to. We'd both come out losers. And it's already starting. I'm feeling guilty and trying to convince myself that maybe I wouldn't hurt you." His jaw clenched. "You're hurting, and offering to change your expectations so that I won't feel guilty. I don't want you to become hard and cynical. I don't want that for you."

"But I still want *you*. More than I've ever wanted anything in my life," she added, laying a conciliatory hand against the warmth of his bare chest.

"Don't do this, Jake," he begged helplessly.

Her inhibitions crashed down around her frozen feet. She curled her toes into the carpet and leaned into him. "I want you, Matt."

He studied her eyes, then seemed to become fascinated with her lips. His drew closer as if pulled by a magnet.

"Please?" she sighed, and his mouth met hers in a bittersweet kiss that felt like goodbye.

She clung to him, loving him with every bit of strength she possessed, willing him to feel her love.

Then she said the dreaded "l" word. She had to tell him how she felt. How could she not say it? He needed to know.

She wasn't surprised when he gently disengaged himself from their tangle. A few minutes later she heard him let himself out her front door.

This time, she knew he wouldn't be back.

CHAPTER TEN

"COME WITH ME, JILLIAN." Karen's voice took on an uncharacteristic whine. "It's only one day. And we're just starting spring break so I refuse to believe you have homework that won't wait."

Jillian attempted to think of yet another way to tell Karen no. Maybe she should try the truth this time; she'd tried everything else. But having finally convinced Karen to leave the subject of Matt alone, Jillian hated to bring him up.

Karen played on her friend's sympathy relentlessly. "Don't make me drive down there by myself."

"What's the matter? If I don't go along with you, you won't be able to practice your verbal arm-twisting, and you'll flunk Badgering the Witness 101?"

Karen lifted one shoulder and said airily, "Something like that."

"You forgot to mention that you want someone to do your dirty work when we get to the other end."

"It's only fair. You were the last one to use the cabin."

Jillian winced. "Matt was," she corrected.

"Which finally brings us to the point. You need to go back and deal with the whole affair."

"It wasn't an affair." She inhaled deeply. "I can't go back, Karen. I can't afford to start that whole miserable merry-go-round again with a trip to memory lane.''

"Going back is just what you need," Karen crowed triumphantly. "Get Matt out of your system once and for all. Put the past behind, face your fears and all that jazz. Why do you think I'm so set on you going? I care about you, Jilly.''

"You've amazed me, starting classes at Washburn, refusing to mope around. But you're determined to stay detached from everything except your books. Everything you do is so emotionless. It's not healthy. You need to do *something* so we can have the old Jilly back. I really miss her, kiddo.''

Jillian shifted uncomfortably.

"A good place to start would be back at the lake. It'll be different there now. The trees will be sprouting tiny buds, the lake is thawed out, there's no snow. You won't even recognize the place." Sensing Jillian's hesitation, Karen continued her coaxing. "All right. How 'bout if I promise not to make you help me? Just keep me company. If it's too painful, cross my heart—" she made the motions "—I'll turn right around and bring you back.''

Jillian looked at her friend's determined expression and gave up her futile attempt to win an argument with a law student—especially this one. She bowed to the inevitable, but not gracefully. "Oh, all right, but don't think you have me fooled. You just want slave labor.''

"You won't be sorry," Karen promised and set off on one of her tangents. "I want you to come to the lake with us this summer. Jim and I have big plans for every weekend, since I have to get out into the real world this fall. I can't stand the thought of you missing all the fun because of some silly hang-up.''

So, that was the legacy from her brief acquaintance with Matt, Jillian mused, Karen's chatter becoming background buzz. A silly hang-up? Funny, it didn't seem so silly.

Could she ever think of her feelings for Matt as silly? Was hurting like crazy silly? At least, thanks to the passage of time, she now felt merely numb.

Karen was right about one thing: it was silly to keep thinking about him. Perhaps Karen was also right about the way to stop.

Jillian glanced over at her friend, who was still talking a mile a minute. What would Karen think if she knew Matt had tried calling her last month? she wondered.

He would have reached her if she hadn't been at one of her classes. Instead, he got the answering machine. She'd trembled when she heard his voice. But since he walked out of her life on New Year's morning, she couldn't think of any sensible reason to renew ''auld acquaintance'' for ''auld lang syne''—and ''auld'' torture. She didn't return the call, she just wondered about it continually. Maybe he wanted to reclaim the small box he'd placed on her kitchen table the night he left.

Or worse! He was probably still feeling guilty and wanted to make sure she hadn't slashed her wrists. The last thing she needed from him was brotherly concern.

If it was important, he would call back. She checked on the safety of John's butterfly earrings obsessively and developed a case of the jitters every time the phone rang.

Somehow, she'd managed to rationalize her inability to throw his number away. One day, in the far, far distant future, she'd call him up and talk happily about her husband and family. And wasn't it a pleasant Christmas they'd shared? And how was *he* doing now?

MAYBE KAREN WAS RIGHT. Maybe coming back here was the way to finally forget Matt, Jillian thought the following Saturday as Karen slowed her little sports car for the last turn. Soon the car was bumping over the deep ruts in the dirt road leading to the cabin. Jillian held her breath.

There was a bittersweet familiarity about everything. As they drove past the rear of the cabin, she picked out the path Matt had taken her along on Christmas Day. A sense of green hinted that spring might soon camouflage it with a wild covering of undergrowth.

The cabin itself looked warm and welcoming. But Jillian was disappointed to see it needed its gilding of icicles and snow to look like the gingerbread house she remembered.

Matt's Blazer, of course, had been perched half-on, half-off the boat ramp leading into the lake instead of on the coarsely graveled clearing. And the lake had glimmered with—

Jillian's head swung back to the dark Blazer. "Oh, no, Karen. Matt's here!"

She expected Karen's expression to reflect her own horror. Instead, Karen grimaced sheepishly.

"You didn't do this to me?"

Karen slid guiltily down in the seat.

Before Karen could defend herself, a sudden movement caught Jillian's eye. The door was open and Matt stood on the edge of the porch, gazing at her. He hesitated for a fraction of a second, then started toward them.

Her heart beat furiously; her throat closed up. Matt smiled tentatively.

Her fingers gripped the edge of the seat and dismay replaced horror. *No,* she protested silently. *I'm not ready. I can't see him now. I'm not nearly as numb as I need to be.*

"Let's get out of here, Karen," she pleaded. Karen smiled like the traitor she was and spread her hands helplessly. Jillian had the insane desire to push her out of the way and make her own tire-squealing, gravel-spraying getaway. Then Matt neared the car and her mind went on hold.

His hair was lighter than she remembered, his complexion a deeper tan. His smile was still tentative, its usual tilt held to a minimum. He was obviously as unnerved as she was.

The door opened, his hand closed around hers and she was out and in his arms. His eyes locked on her mouth.

Jillian told herself to pull away, but something held her. Something other than his light grasp and her own longing to meet his lips. She had to know why he was here.

A real smile spread slowly across his face and his tiger's eyes seemed to dance.

"Thanks, Karen," he said without looking in her direction, without letting Jillian go. He leaned against the door, closing it with his hip, and Karen put the car in reverse.

"But—"

Matt stopped her protest by covering her mouth with his.

"I'll take you anywhere you want to go," he promised against her lips, and she was lost.

She gave herself up to the forgetfulness induced by his kiss until he swung her up into his arms and would have carried her to the cabin.

"I can't do this again, Matt," she sighed wearily against his neck.

"Do what?" He placed a butterfly kiss on the corner of her mouth, then set her down.

Jillian shook her head, unable to put her feelings into words. She couldn't start the whole healing process over again. She couldn't do it.

"I didn't *want* to hurt you."

She needed to strike back. "But you did," she whispered. "I can't go through it all again."

"I love you, Jillian. Does that make a difference?"

"You loved me then." He started to say something, so she rushed on. "Even if you didn't admit it, I felt it. And it didn't make a difference then."

Matt leaned back. "I don't have the strength to fight it anymore." He hugged her close again. "And it scares the hell out of me sometimes, Jake."

He tried to lead her toward the cabin, but she held back.

"I'll drive you to Topeka the minute you say the word," he promised. "I just want to talk. Hear me out. Please?"

She considered his request, then nodded. "But let's walk."

"All right."

He clasped her hand and they headed for the path.

"The initial construction is almost done on my little village," he said after they'd gone a short way. "I already have two craftsmen in residence and plan to open this summer."

"I'm glad," Jillian replied sincerely. He sounded so excited and happy.

"It's all coming together as if it were meant to be. The weather even cooperated during crucial times."

That's nice, she thought, *but what does it have to do with me?* They walked silently for a few minutes.

"I have an advertising firm working on a national campaign. They're putting out some initial publicity next week."

They had reached a small clearing where the lake lapped noisily at the muddy shoreline. "It looks a little different now, doesn't it?" he murmured.

She could feel the barrier around her heart cracking and melting like the ice on the lake, and she didn't like it. "If you had Karen bring me here to give me an update on your progress," she said wryly, "it wasn't necessary. Jim had felt obligated to keep me informed." She'd listened hungrily during those first few weeks of the new year. But with the blessed onslaught of numbness, she'd gradually trained herself to ignore Jim's commentaries. The longer she was with

Matt now, the more she'd allow her hopes to rise—and that was *all* they were—hopes. Pipe dreams.

She sat down primly on a sun-warmed rock and looked at him impatiently. "What's the point of all this?"

Matt leaned against a tree, one knee bent sharply, his foot resting on the trunk. "I'm getting to that," he said.

Jillian read the uncertainty in his eyes and forced herself to wait.

"I've been slowly rebuilding my life. Till now, I've been content to wander from place to place, store to store."

"I don't see what that has to do with me."

"I didn't either, at first. I almost turned down the initial offer to sell without thinking about it, because every time I spent more than a couple of weeks in one place, I got restless. By the time you left here after Christmas, I knew I wanted out, but was hesitant to make a decision." He shrugged. "I didn't know what I would do if I went ahead."

"And then you remembered about the artists' colony."

He shook his head. "Not right away. I was too busy finding a reason to come to Topeka and see you. I decided—well, you know what I decided. I decided to sell so I'd have an excuse to ask you to help me celebrate."

Jillian's eyes widened in amazement.

"I was afraid you and Harrison might have made up your differences and I had to know. I told myself it was because I felt protective of you, like a brother. I figured I would disappear back into the woodwork once I was sure you were happy and that would be that. I didn't remember the colony until you questioned me at the restaurant." He shifted nervously. "I rattled the whole thing off the top of my head. Made up details, even. I didn't want you to suspect I didn't have the slightest idea what I was going to do after I took you home that night."

Jillian didn't want to think about that night. And she didn't want Matt to see the pain in her eyes. She rose and wandered to the lake's muddy edge.

"When I left Topeka New Year's morning, I couldn't stop thinking I should take you with me to Colorado."

She felt him come to stand behind her.

"I knew you wouldn't just live with me," he went on. "That meant marriage, and I felt trapped."

"And angry at me for laying the trap," Jillian added.

"Angry at myself for even considering it," he corrected. His hands covered her shoulders and he turned her to face him. "I was afraid of what marriage to me would do to you. Afraid any changes it made in me wouldn't be good ones. I'm not good—"

"Good husband material," she finished for him and backed away into the mud. "Oh, damn," she choked out as her foot sank. Relieved at the diversion, she braced a hand on his shoulder and raised her leg. Her shoe stayed in the mucky silt.

"Let me." Matt lifted her and set her farther up the bank onto dry ground. She stood like a flamingo while he bent to pull her loafer free.

She kept her head down as he scraped the heavy mud from her shoe. "There," he said, glancing up.

"Please don't cry, Jake." He dropped the shoe and took her in his arms.

"I can't help it," she whispered. "Nothing's changed. I can't forget everything I was brought up to believe in and you aren't good husband material...." She swiped at her tears with the back of her hand.

"Things *have* changed. That's what I'm trying to tell you." Matt picked her up. "You're going to have us both sprawled in the mud if you keep standing there on one foot, crying." He carried her over to the rock and sat down, cradling her on his lap.

"I don't see—"

"Just listen," he begged gently, hushing her with a kiss.

She peeped up at him warily.

"When I left Topeka New Year's morning, I headed for Colorado like a demon was after me. I didn't intend to ever set foot in this part of the country again, so I *had* to sell the stores. I kept my mind off you by thinking about the colony. I knew it was what I wanted to do the minute I told you about it. I suddenly wanted a permanent base. By the time I got home, it was just a matter of calling the right people and putting everything in motion." He looked at her sheepishly. "I thought I'd fixed everything and could put you out of my mind, but every step of the way, I caught myself thinking, 'Jillian would like this,' or 'I can hardly wait for Jake to see that.'"

Jillian held her breath.

"And now I *have* fixed everything," he assured her gently. "I've fixed it so you fit into my life. I want you to see it all," he added huskily. "I want you to share it with me. Will you think about it?"

"Oh, Matt." Tears were streaming down her cheeks again.

"I hope these are happy tears." He smiled wiping one away as she threw her arms around him enthusiastically.

Waves of happiness washed over her as she kissed the tiny, erratic pulse behind his ear and let her hand slowly verify that he was solid and real.

He sighed as though the weight of the world had been lifted. "You have to quit doing that if we're going to talk," he said at last, putting her firmly away from him. He set her on the rock and reached for her shoe. "Shall I play Prince Charming?"

"No." She gently took the shoe from him and put it on her own foot. "I've been expecting fairy-tale endings long enough," she said soberly. "If anything is going to work between us, we both have to be practical."

He buried his face in her windswept hair. "I wish I could take back all the hurt."

She couldn't hold down a low bubbling laugh. "I'm healing fast."

He drew her to her feet, slipping his hands into her back pockets. She gave him a long and thoroughly satisfying kiss.

"Enough," he said. "We have to make plans like intelligent adults and I can't think when you do that."

She smiled and started to step away. He tugged her toward him by her back pockets and kissed her till her toes curled. "I love you," he whispered into her parted lips.

"I've waited forever to hear you say that." She breathed the words against his mouth.

"Now, we have to decide what we're going to do with the rest of our lives. Starting with Monday," he added, stealing a quick kiss from her. "I *know* what we're going to do with the rest of the weekend, if you'll agree."

She grinned in response and felt absolutely, wickedly wonderful.

"Shall we have a big wedding?"

The brightness went out of the lovely day. "Don't, Matt," she pleaded softly.

She kept her gaze on a slender branch that had been a victim of the wind. Its tiny buds once promised a future. Now it was lying on the ground, dry and shriveled. "I wouldn't do that to you." She tried to disguise the hurt in her voice.

"Do you honestly think I could've got Karen to go along with this abduction if I didn't have marriage in mind?"

"But I don't want you to feel like I've trapped you or, or... *made* you marry me." She held his eyes, longing for him to understand that, as far as she was concerned, his love was enough.

"I want, repeat, *want* to marry you, my sweet Jillian." His lips were inches from hers. "I don't have the excuse anymore that my life wouldn't accommodate a wife."

Her eyes glittered with a new crop of tears.

"Do you want me to go through life as alone as I've always been?"

She shook her head.

"If you marry me, will I ever have to lie awake wondering how you're passing the night?"

A tender smile grew as she shook her head again.

"I didn't sleep for days after I called you and you were still out at ten-thirty."

"I wasn't home from class yet," she assured him.

"I know that now. Karen told me when we cooked up this kidnapping. But at the time, I had visions of old Harry and any number of other guys beating your door down. It was hell."

"I'm sorry." She glowed, looking up at him and stroking his face.

"I want you to be my friend, and—"

"I already am." She was finally convinced that he really wanted to marry her, but she wanted to hear all his reasons. Her smile grew broader.

"And I want you to be my lover."

"I'm willing," she sighed contentedly.

He gently tweaked her nose. "Will you promise forever?"

Her breathing slowed as her heart rate picked up. She searched frantically for the right words.

"See? You won't promise, so I'll need some sort of legal guarantee...."

"You said there *are* no guarantees," she pointed out.

"Nevertheless, I want to make it as hard for you to get rid of me as I possibly can. Which brings me back to my previous question: Do you want a big wedding?"

"No."

"Good," he said. "I didn't especially want one either. I'm kind of partial to a justice of the peace in the closest place we can find without a waiting period."

"A minister, maybe?" she asked hopefully.

He mulled that one over.

"It'll be much more binding that way, don't you think?" she teased, afraid that if she said it as seriously as she felt it, he'd reject the whole idea.

"Maybe we'll get two." He held her so tightly she feared she might break. She couldn't think. He kissed her until she didn't want to.

Later, much later, he held her hand as they sat on the porch steps and watched the moon rise.

"Matt?"

"Yes?"

"Does this plan include any babies?"

He laughed softly, then broke into the roar of delighted amusement she loved so much. It echoed through the trees, startling the few night creatures who had ventured out of their hiding places early.

"It's not funny."

"I know, Jillian," he said lovingly, as he drew her across his lap. "But can we take one step at a time? I'm still trying to figure out what a good husband does."

"He acts like you." She said adoringly. Smoothing the disbelieving lines away from his forehead with her fingertip, she explained, "He gives love."

He kissed the tip of her nose reverently. "Thanks, sweetheart. If it's that easy, I've got it made. And if I do all right with this?" In the growing darkness, she felt his shoulders lift in the familiar shrug. "Who knows? Maybe we'll try the other."

She heard Grandma's contented sigh on a whisper of wind. "Yes," she agreed, raising her face to kiss him. "Who knows?"

You'll flip . . . your pages won't!
Read paperbacks *hands-free* with

Book Mate·I

The perfect "mate" for all your romance paperbacks

Traveling • Vacationing • At Work • In Bed • Studying • Cooking • Eating

Perfect size for all standard paperbacks, this wonderful invention makes reading a pure pleasure! Ingenious design holds paperback books OPEN and FLAT so even wind can't ruffle pages— leaves your hands free to do other things. Reinforced, wipe-clean vinyl-covered holder flexes to let you turn pages without undoing the strap . . . supports paperbacks so well, they have the strength of hardcovers!

Pages turn WITHOUT opening the strap.

SEE-THROUGH STRAP

Reinforced back stays flat

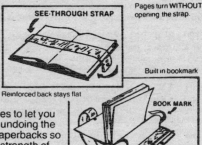

Built in bookmark

BOOK MARK

BACK COVER HOLDING STRIP

10" x 7¼" . opened.
Snaps closed for easy carrying, too.

Available now. Send your name, address, and zip code, along with a check or money order for just $5.95 + .75¢ for delivery (for a total of $6.70) payable to Reader Service to:

Reader Service
Bookmate Offer
3010 Walden Avenue
P.O. Box 1396
Buffalo, N.Y. 14269-1396

Offer not available in Canada
*New York residents add appropriate sales tax.

BM-GR

HARLEQUIN
American Romance®

RELIVE THE MEMORIES. . . .

From New York's immigrant experience to San Francisco's great quake of 1906. From the muddy trenches of World War I's western front to the speakeasies of the Roaring Twenties. From the lost fortunes and indomitable spirit of the Thirties to life on the home front in the Fabulous Forties...**A CENTURY OF AMERICAN ROMANCE** takes you on a nostalgic journey through the twentieth century.

Glimpse the lives and loves of American men and women from the turn of the century to the dawn of the year 2000. Revel in the romance of a time gone by. And sneak a peek at romance in an exciting future.

Watch for all the **A CENTURY OF AMERICAN ROMANCE** titles coming to you one per month in Harlequin American Romance.

Don't miss a day of **A CENTURY OF AMERICAN ROMANCE**.

A CENTURY OF AMERICAN ROMANCE

1960s

The women . . . the men . . . the passions . . . the memories. . . .